Praise for *Amina's Voice*

★"Amina's middle school woes and the universal themes
running through the book transcend culture, race, and religion.
A perfect first book for this new Muslim imprint."
—*Kirkus Reviews*, starred review

★"A universal story of self-acceptance and the acceptance of
others. A welcome addition to any middle grade collection."
—*School Library Journal*, starred review

★"Written as beautifully as Amina's voice surely is,
this compassionate, timely novel is highly recommended."
—*Booklist*, starred review

"Amina's anxieties are entirely relatable, but it's her sweet-hearted
nature that makes her such a winning protagonist."
—*Entertainment Weekly*

"Watching Amina literally and figuratively find her voice—
bolstered by community, friendship, and discovered inner
strength—makes for rewarding reading."
—*Publishers Weekly*

"[A] gentle coming-of-age story universal in theme and
original in context, and appealing to any reader who has just
wanted to slow the world down."
—*Shelf Awareness*

Amina's Voice

Hena Khan

New York • London • Toronto • Sydney • New Delhi

An imprint of Simon & Schuster Children's Publishing Division
1230 Avenue of the Americas, New York, New York 10020
This book is a work of fiction. Any references to historical events, real people, or real places are used fictitiously. Other names, characters, places, and events are products of the author's imagination, and any resemblance to actual events or places or persons, living or dead, is entirely coincidental.

For information about special discounts for bulk purchases, please contact Simon & Schuster Special Sales at 1-866-506-1949 or business@simonandschuster.com.
The Simon & Schuster Speakers Bureau can bring authors to your live event. For more information or to book an event, contact the Simon & Schuster Speakers Bureau at 1-866-248-3049 or visit our website at www.simonspeakers.com.
Cover design by Krista Vossen
Interior design by Hilary Zarycky
The text for this book was set in Adobe Garamond Pro.
Manufactured in the United States of America
1118 OFF
First SALAAM READS paperback edition May 2018
Also available as a Salaam Reads hardcover edition
6 8 10 9 7 5
The Library of Congress has cataloged the hardcover edition as follows:
Names: Khan, Hena, author.
Title: Amina's voice / Hena Khan.
Description: First edition. | New York : Salaam Reads / Simon & Schuster Books for Young Readers, [2017] | Summary: "A Pakistani-American Muslim girl struggles to stay true to her family's vibrant culture while simultaneously blending in at school after tragedy strikes her community"— Provided by publisher.
Identifiers: LCCN 2016024621| ISBN 9781481492065 (hardcover) | ISBN 9781481492072 (pbk)| ISBN 9781481492089 (eBook)
Subjects: LCSH: Muslims—Juvenile fiction. | Pakistani Americans—Juvenile fiction. | CYAC: Muslims—Fiction. | Pakistani Americans—Fiction. | Friendship—Fiction. | BISAC: JUVENILE FICTION / Family / General (see also headings under Social Issues). | JUVENILE FICTION / Social Issues / Friendship. | JUVENILE FICTION / Social Issues / Prejudice & Racism.
Classification: LCC PZ7.K526495 Am 2017 | DDC [Fic]—dc23
LC record available at https://lccn.loc.gov/2016024621

For my father, a true gentleman,
who is missed every day for his soft voice,
intellectual curiosity, and generous spirit.

ACKNOWLEDGMENTS

Writing *Amina's Voice* also meant finding my own along the way, with the help of many special people. I'm enormously grateful to Andrea Menotti, friend, editor, and gifted storyteller, for launching me onto the children's writing stage and continuing to guide me over the years. You are the best. I was fortunate to have talented author Naheed H. Senzai swap chapters with me during the first draft of the book and offer valuable insights. Two bright young reviewers, Jenna Din and Imaan Shanavas, gave me their honest assessments early on in the process. Afgen Sheikh was a huge support, as he carefully read each revision, talked me through my dialogue, and challenged me to make the story considerably better. My critique group, Laura Gehl, Ann McCallum, and Joan Waites, articulated what was missing in order to make Amina a stronger character when no one else quite could.

I want to express heartfelt appreciation for my agent, Matthew Elblonk, for believing in the importance of this story, and for working hard to find it a home. And a huge thank-you to editor Zareen Jaffery for both championing it and making it part of a groundbreaking effort in children's publishing. I'm so proud to join the passionate team at Salaam Reads.

A number of other dear friends have cheered me on, listened to my whining, and celebrated my victories over the time it took to get this book published. You know who you are, and I couldn't have done it without you. My parents and siblings always encouraged my writing, but my mother, Zahida Khan, is the one who instilled a love for books and reading in me at a young age. Everything I am is because of your tireless efforts. Finally, my husband, Farrukh, and two sons, Bilal and Humza, are my biggest fans and source of joy. Thank you for pushing me to pursue my dreams, for being patient with me, and for inspiring me every day.

Amina's Voice

1

Something sharp pokes me in the rib.

"You should totally sign up for a solo," Soojin whispers from the seat behind me in music class.

I shake my head. The mere thought of singing in front of a crowd makes my stomach twist into knots.

"But you're such a good singer," Soojin insists.

I pause, enjoying the praise for a second. Soojin is the only one at school who knows I can sing, and she thinks I'm amazing at it. Every Tuesday we argue about the best contestant on *The Voice* and who deserves to advance to the next round. I can count on Soojin to end the conversation by saying that I'm better than most of the people on the show, and that I deserve to be on it someday. But what she doesn't consider is that if by some miracle I was standing in front of the judges and live studio audience, I wouldn't be able to croak out a word. I shake my head again.

"Come on, Amina. Just try it." Soojin is a little louder now.

"Girls, is that chatter about you volunteering?" Ms. Holly stares at us from the front of the classroom with her eyebrows raised.

"Ouch!" I yelp. It's Soojin's pencil in my side again.

"Is that a yes, Amina? Should I sign you up for a solo for the concert?" Ms. Holly asks. "How about one of the Motown pieces from the 1970s?"

I sink lower into my chair as everyone stares at me and stumble over my words. "Um, no, thank you. I'll just stay in the chorus," I finally manage to mutter.

"Okay." Ms. Holly shrugs, a frown clouding her face until Julie Zawacki, waving her hand like an overenthusiastic first grader, distracts her. Julie always wants the spotlight and tends to sing extremely loudly. It's as if she thinks volume makes up for her lack of pitch. I always wonder how the math class next door gets any work done whenever Julie starts belting. But I still wish I had even half the guts she does.

"Remember, we've only got two months to prepare for the Winter Choral Concert. This is a big deal, guys," Ms. Holly calls out as the bell rings and we file out for lunch.

"I can't believe you didn't sign up," Soojin complains as we sit down at what has already become our usual spot in the lunchroom three weeks into the school year. "This is your big chance to finally show everyone what you've been hiding."

I'm pretty sure that was what Adam, the judge with sleeve tattoos, said to the tall redheaded girl on *The Voice* last Sunday night, and I tell her that.

"I'm serious," Soojin says. "It's time to forget about John Hancock."

Just the mention of that name brings back the memories I've tried to block since second grade: our class play about American independence. I was John Hancock and

3

was supposed to say one line: "I will proudly sign my name in big letters." But when it came time for the performance, I looked out into the audience, saw the sea of faces, and froze. There was this endless moment when the world grew still and waited for me to speak. But I couldn't open my mouth. My teacher, Mr. Silver, finally jumped in and said my line for me, with a joke about how John Hancock had lost his voice but was going to sign his name extra big to make up for it. The audience laughed and the show went on while I burned with humiliation. I can still hear Luke and his friend jeering at me from the side of the stage.

"That was forever ago! We're in sixth grade now. You need to get over it." Soojin sighs as if my entire middle school future depends on performing a solo in Ms. Holly's Blast from the Past production. I don't let her see how much I agree with her and how badly I want the spot.

"Anyway, do you think I look like a Heidi?" she continues.

I have a mouthful of sandwich and stare at her as I chew, relieved that she's changed the subject. I try to imagine her with a name I associate with Swiss cartoon characters or a famous supermodel—not my twelve-year-old Korean best friend.

"Not really," I finally say after swallowing. "Why?"

"What about Jessica? Do I look like a Jessica?" Soojin picks carrots out of an overstuffed sandwich wrapped in white deli paper.

"No. What are you talking about?"

"I got it." Soojin sits back and crosses her arms. She's hardly reassembled her sandwich and it's already half gone. No one I know eats as fast as Soojin. It's one of the many ways we are opposites. I can't ever finish my lunch, no matter how hard I try.

"What?"

"Melanie! I *totally* feel like a Melanie, and I love that name." Soojin flips her long black hair off her shoulder and acts like she is meeting me for the first time. "Hi, I'm Melanie."

"What's wrong with you? Are you feeling okay?"

Soojin pretends to pout. "Just tell me, who *do* you think I look like?"

"Soo-jin," I say slowly. I put the other half of my sandwich back into my bag and pull mini pretzels out. "You look exactly like a Soojin."

Soojin sighs again, extra loudly, just like she does when her younger sister pesters us to play with her. It seems like I'm getting that sigh more and more lately—ever since the start of middle school. "That's because you've always known me as Soojin, Amina."

"Yeah, that's my point."

"What's your point?" I hear a familiar voice behind me and turn around. A small, blond girl is carrying a cafeteria tray and a jumbo metal water bottle with the words "I am not PLASTIC" on it. *Emily.* Her green eyes and tiny nose remind me of my next-door neighbor's bad-tempered cat, Smokey.

"Nothing," I say. I wait for her to keep walking to the other side of the lunchroom, where she always sits with Julie and her crew.

"What are you guys talking about?" she asks.

I wait for Soojin to answer, expecting her to say something to send Emily scurrying. Even though the cat gets my tongue when either Emily or Julie come prowling, Soojin never has any problem telling them exactly what she thinks.

But Soojin just says, "I'm thinking of new names for myself."

"New names? That's weird. Why?" Emily starts a stream of questions. And as much as I want Emily to leave, I want to hear the answers.

"It's not weird at all, actually. My family and I are becoming citizens soon, and I'm going to change my name."

"Wait. So that means you're not even *American*?" Emily sounds offended.

"What?" I ask. There is no way I heard Soojin right. "Change your name? What for?"

Soojin smooths her hair, sips some fizzy juice, and takes a deep breath. "We moved from Korea when I was four, and we aren't American citizens yet. But we are about to be, and I'm going to change my name. I just haven't picked one yet."

"Oh, I have the perfect name for you," Emily volunteers. She plops down her tray on the table and smiles like

7

she is about to spill a juicy secret. "Fiona," she says.

"Fiona?" I snort. "As in the green ogre girl from the *Shrek* movies?"

"No. Fiona, as in my uncle's Scottish girlfriend. She's totally pretty."

I flash Soojin a look, but she doesn't notice. Instead, she actually seems to be pondering the name as if it's a possibility. An *ogre* name! Suggested by Emily!

And then Emily suddenly starts to shove herself into the space next to me. I don't move at first. But when she's nearly in my lap and Soojin still doesn't say anything, I scoot over to make just enough room for her. Then I lean across the table and stare hard at Soojin.

Why is Emily sitting with us?

Ever since before Soojin moved to Greendale from New York in third grade, Emily has worked extremely hard to be Julie's best friend. Mama would say Emily was Julie's chamchee, which means "spoon" in Urdu. That doesn't make a lot of sense, except that it also means "suck-up." And Emily has always sucked up to Julie, even if that means laughing really hard at her dumb jokes or chiming in when she puts everyone else down. And by everyone else, I mean mostly Soojin and me.

"Fi-oh-na," Soojin repeats. "That's kind of nice."

"Do you like it?" Emily asks me.

"Not—um—I don't know," I stammer. "Do you *seriously* think she looks like a Fiona?"

"*Duh*. She can look like anybody she wants, can't she?" Emily turns back to Soojin.

My face grows hot.

"Don't you like being Soojin?" I ask my best friend in a low voice, leaning across the table to make it harder for Emily to hear. "You've been Soojin your whole life. Aren't you used to it?" I want to add that we had always been the only kids in elementary school with names that everyone stumbled over. That is, until Olayinka came along in fifth grade. It's always been one of our "things."

"Really, Amina? I thought you, at least, would understand what it's like to have people mess up your name every single day." Soojin lets out her sigh again. And this time it feels like I deserve it, even though I don't know why.

Mama told me once that she picked my name thinking it would be easiest of all the ones on her list for people in America to pronounce. But she was wrong. The neighbor with the creepy cat still calls me Amelia after living next door for five years. And my last name? Forget about it. I could barely pronounce Khokar myself until I was at least eight. And since I don't want to embarrass anyone by correcting them more than once, I just let them say my name any way they want.

Soojin is the only one at school who gets it. Whenever a substitute teacher pauses during roll call and asks, "Oh, ah, how do you say your name, dear?" I don't even have to look at her to know she's rolling her eyes. We still collapse into giggling fits if one of us mentions the lady who called me Anemia, as in the blood disorder. But now all of a sudden Soojin wants to be a Fiona or a Heidi?

Does it have something to do with being in middle school?

"What other names do you like?" Emily asks. She's so interested in the conversation that she hasn't touched the limp grilled cheese sandwich on her tray yet. I lean back and chew my pretzels while Soojin repeats her other choices to Emily.

"Ooh. I like Melanie, too," Emily says. As I watch them chat, the lunchroom starts to feel like someone's cranked up the heat. My palms get sweaty, and I feel super thirsty, and not just from the pretzels. I look around and find Julie sitting at her usual table, talking with a couple of new girls from another elementary school. She doesn't seem to even notice that Emily is missing. I don't say another word until Emily gets up to put her tray away and go to the bathroom before the bell rings.

"Soojin's a pretty name too," I say in as normal a voice as I can. "And I'm not just saying it because I'm used to it." I want to add that I can't imagine calling Soojin any of those other names, and that it would feel like I was talking to an impostor—but I don't. It doesn't seem like Soojin wants to hear that.

"Thanks." Soojin's face softens. "You know, a lot of Korean people have two names, a Korean one and an English one."

"Yeah. But you didn't have another name before. So why do you want one now?"

"I always wished I had a different name. Besides, my whole family is picking new ones."

Soojin's dad already goes by George and her mom is Mary, so their names would just become official after they take the oath to become citizens. I call them Mr. and Mrs. Park anyway, since my parents never let me call any grown-ups by their first names. Everyone is Auntie and Uncle or Mr. and Mrs. But Soojin taking on a new name just doesn't seem right.

"Can I still call you Soojin?" I ask after swallowing hard to clear the lump that has formed in my throat.

"I want everyone to use my new name and get used to it in middle school, so it's normal when we get to high school. It would be messed up if my own best friend didn't do it." Soojin peers into my face expectantly. "You will, right?"

"Yeah. I will," I promise, although I cross my toes inside my shoes. I decide I will call her Soojin for as long as possible. The knots tighten in my stomach again, churning the half sandwich, seven mini pretzels, and three bites of cookie sitting inside. I watch Soojin put her empty containers back in her lunch bag, looking for a clue to why she's acting so bizarre. Because even though I can't explain why, something about Soojin wanting to drop her name makes me worry that I might be next.

2

I spot Baba's car pulling up outside the music school building and stuff my song sheets into my folder.

"You nailed it, Amina. We'll pick a new song next week," Mrs. Kuckleman says. Her face has been smiling for the past six years that I've been pounding on the yellowed keys of the Tony Fritz Music Center's piano every week. It wasn't long after I started lessons that Mrs. Kuckleman told my parents that I have perfect pitch, since I can recognize any musical note. They were overjoyed—especially Baba, who loves the word "perfect" when it applies to his kids.

"How's my geeta?" Baba asks as I scramble into the backseat before the car behind us has a chance to honk. My father says he calls me geeta, or "song," because even my newborn crying was to the theme of his favorite Bollywood movie, *Kuch Kuch Hota Hai*.

"Really hungry," I say. "Where's Mama?"

My mom usually picks me up, since Baba's schedule is so unpredictable.

"She's at your school for the back-to-school night. We are going now."

"*We?* I'm not supposed to go! It's only for parents. Can't you drop me home first?"

"No, no, there's no time." Baba shakes his head. "It's fine. You can wait in the hallway."

I want to explain to my father that it would be completely embarrassing to be the only kid tagging along with her parents at back-to-school night. But he would just say, in the Urdu accent he hasn't lost after living in the Milwaukee area for twenty years, "Embarrassing? I don't understand this embarrassing. Why do you care what people think?"

"It's okay. You don't have to go. Mama's already there," I plead. "You must be tired."

"Your mother wants me to go. And there's only half an hour left. It's settled."

I don't argue further and sink into my seat, glad for a change that Baba doesn't allow me to sit in the front so I can sulk in peace. I've been begging him to let me, since I'm turning twelve in five months, but he hears too many stories about air-bag disasters from the trauma team he works with at the hospital. And since I haven't reached the recommended minimum age on the air-bag warning sticker, and since I barely weigh eighty pounds, I'm lucky he doesn't force me into a booster seat.

We get to school in time for the last three classes, since there are only ten minutes allotted for teachers to summarize their lessons. By the last session, I honestly don't know who's wishing more that we hadn't shown up—me or Mrs. Gardner. Maybe Baba is trying to make up for being late, but he won't stop asking questions.

"So these experiments, will they include lab work?"

All the other parents are shifting in their seats and checking their phones. I look at Mama, trying to will her to control my father. But Mama is beaming with pride over her husband's interest in my education.

"And that wraps up back-to-school night," Mrs. Gardner finally says after answering Baba's last question and ignoring him when he raises his hand again. "Thank you for coming. We've had a successful first three weeks of school. If you have any other questions, please e-mail me." Then she hurries to the back of the room, grabs a bag from the closet, and ushers us out the door.

"Your teachers seem nice. But it sounds like you'll have a lot of work," Baba says on the way home. He pulls into the driveway and turns around to face me, dark eyes serious. "You must study very hard in middle school. You see what happened to your brother?"

"I know, Baba." My older brother was a star student in elementary school. But once he got to middle school, Mustafa's grades went downhill. Since he started high school this year, dinner often becomes lectures about how Mustafa needs to "get serious." And a few nights ago, when they thought I was in bed, I heard my parents talking about him getting "out of control like those American boys."

"I *am* American," Mustafa likes to remind them, whenever they say something like that to him. Sometimes he even mutters, "If you didn't want American children, you shouldn't have moved to this country," but usually only loud enough for me to hear.

"Hey, guys," Mustafa says as we walk through the garage door. He's sprawled on the old sectional with the television remote.

"We aren't *guys*. Is it so hard to say salaam properly to your parents?" Mama grumbles while I put my shoes away. Her accent, along with her complexion, is a bit lighter than Baba's, and people have a hard time guessing that she's from Pakistan.

I smile as I remember that "guy" in Urdu is the word for "cow." Mustafa winks at me as Mama goes into the kitchen to warm dinner. *Mustafa's in a good mood, so maybe we can eat in peace.*

"How was back-to-school night?" Mustafa asks as we sit down at the table. "Who'd you get for homeroom?"

"Ms. Bixler." I don't hide my surprise that he's asking. My brother doesn't usually act like he cares a whole lot about me or what I'm doing. When he isn't watching TV, he's texting his friends or pushing past me in the hallway to go to his room and close the door.

"Is she new? I don't remember her," Mustafa continues, chewing.

"Yeah, I think she started last year." If Mustafa had Ms. Bixler, she would have probably asked me, "Khokar? Are you related to Mustafa?" on the first day of school. Our last name is an obvious giveaway, and I'm used to being linked to him. But now I don't know what to say when his old teachers ask how he is doing. I figure they don't want to hear about the C he got on his science test or how he was grounded for the past two weeks for talking back. So I just stick with, "He's fine."

"Did you finish your homework?" Mama asks Mustafa.

"I did it all at school. Don't worry, Ma," Mustafa replies with a mouthful of chickpea masala. It has too many onions in it, and I push my food around on my plate with my naan, wishing I were eating the rest of my peanut butter sandwich from lunch instead.

"We won't worry when we see all As on your report card." Baba clears his throat like he always does when he's extra serious. "You are in high school now, Mustafa, and it's not a joke."

"I know, Baba. Relax, the school year just started." Mustafa puts down his fork, his head lowered, and I brace myself for another argument.

But as Baba wipes his plate, Mustafa jumps out of his seat, stacks the dirty dishes, and carries them over to the sink. Then he puts water in the kettle and takes out the tin of tea leaves for making chai, instead of going back to the couch.

What does he want?

"So I was talking to my guidance counselor about college and how I need some extracurricular activities," he says while loading dishes into the washer.

"Did she suggest mathematics club or science club?" Baba asks. "That would be great for getting into medical school."

"No, actually, I was thinking of trying out for the basketball team."

"Basketball?" Baba frowns. "No, no. Why basketball? Timothy next door says his son is captain of the chess team. You should do that."

"But I'm good at ball, not chess, Baba." Mustafa drops the silverware into the dishwasher with a clang. "My gym teacher thinks I have a good shot at making JV as a freshman."

"Basketball will be a distraction from schoolwork," Baba says. His brow wrinkles. "Your grades should be your number one priority."

"But my counselor says I have to be well-rounded to get into a good college. Good grades aren't everything."

It sounds like Mustafa has been thinking about what to say. I notice the line of stubble on his jaw. Recently, it's like the brother I've known my entire life has vanished, and a total stranger—one with better hygiene—has moved into his place. For years Mama begged him to at least wash his face in the morning and even got him special men's woodsy-scented foaming face cleanser, but he didn't touch it. And now Mustafa practically lives in the bathroom, shaves, gels his hair, and drowns in cologne. The weirdest part of it all is Soojin saying that she overheard girls on her bus talking about how "cute" he is.

Gross. There is only one way I can think of Mustafa as cute. In the photo that sits on the mantel in the family room, there's a four-year-old version of him in a bow tie with a face covered in blue birthday-cake icing.

"Do they have sofas at basketball practice?" Mama chimes in. "All you want to do is lie down and watch TV all the time."

"Come on, Ma." Mustafa hangs his head.

"And what about the driving? Who's going to take you and bring you from practices and games? You know what time we get home."

"Plus there's Sunday school too," I blurt out. But I wish I could take it back when Mustafa shoots me a death glare.

"Yes, your sister is right. School and Sunday school have to come first," Baba agrees.

Mustafa looks helplessly around the room, frustration growing in his eyes.

I better do something.

I slide out of my seat and stand next to Baba, giving him a quick kiss on the cheek. He rests his hand on my shoulder, and after I take a deep breath, I speak up. "You know, Soojin's cousin got into Harvard, and she said it was because he was the captain of his basketball team."

"Harvard? The real Harvard? He must have good SATs also?"

"Yeah, the real one. All I know is he was really good at basketball. Soojin said that her whole family couldn't believe he got in because he's not even smart."

"Is that so?" Baba muses. "Basketball?"

"Here's the permission form for tryouts," Mustafa says quickly, giving me a slight nod to acknowledge my effort. "Please think about it." He pulls a folded paper out of his pocket and places it on the table.

"Okay, we'll see," Baba says. He clears his throat again, this time to signal he is done with that conversation. "Guess who I spoke to today?"

"Who?" I ask.

"Your Thaya Jaan." Baba's voice deepens as he utters the

23

title that means "dear older brother of my father." "He is coming to visit."

"Acha?" Mama's eyes widen. "They actually gave him a visa?"

I try to picture my uncle, who I haven't seen since I was six years old, the only time I've ever been to Pakistan. I have fuzzy memories of the trip: a large house with a green metal gate, and a guard in front, and a big buffalo in the backyard. But I really only know Thaya Jaan as a grainy figure on Skype who my parents make me say salaam to from time to time.

"Yes. He sounded very happy," Baba says. He clears his throat before continuing. "His visa is for three months, so he'll be here for a while."

We all glance at Mama to see how she will react to having someone from my dad's family stay with us for so long.

"When does he arrive?" Mama looks in Baba's direction, but she doesn't wait for an answer. "We have to get the house fixed before. The garage has to be clean—I want all of those boxes out." Mama rattles off more tasks in super-hostess mode. But then she stops midsentence and points at Mustafa and me with a warning look. "And you two better behave. No fighting and no being rude."

"That's right," Baba says. "I want my brother to see that my kids are just as disciplined as his and that I made the right decision to settle here. I don't think he's ever forgiven me for not returning to Pakistan."

"What do you mean?" I ask.

"My brother always thought I'd come back after my residency. But I didn't." Baba's eyes grow thoughtful. "You know I was only a couple of years older than you, Mustafa, when my father died and your uncle took care of me. I respect him so much that if he told me it was day outside when it was night, I would agree."

"That makes no sense—" Mustafa starts to argue before Mama shushes him.

"That's the way respect works. No talking back. Remember what I said. You two better be *perfect*."

Mustafa and I exchange grimaces. Even though I'm happy for Baba that his brother is finally coming to

America, he's basically a stranger to me. And three months is an awfully long time to have a guest live in our house, especially someone who is never wrong. Plus, it's going to seem like a whole lot longer if we all have to pretend to be perfect the entire time.

3

"Settle down and take your seats, everyone," commands Mrs. Barton after the bell rings. She stands with her hands on her hips, dressed in a ruffled shirt with a high collar and a long skirt. "Today we are beginning our new unit on the pioneers of the American West."

"Is that why you're wearing that?" Luke says it like he's sincerely interested, but everyone except for Mrs. Barton knows he's making fun of her.

"Yes, exactly. This outfit is just like the ones pioneers used to wear in the mid-1800s. You all need to get into character because you're going to race across the country to Oregon by wagon train in teams of four!"

"Wait, so we have to dress up?" Bradley asks in a worried voice.

"No, Bradley." Mrs. Barton sighs. "What I mean is you have to pretend you are a pioneer and think like one. We're doing a modified version of the classic Oregon Trail game. I was telling your parents last night that in this project you'll learn how to overcome challenges like food shortages, natural disasters, and diseases."

I'm sitting at the desk next to Soojin, and I nod at her and mouth, "We got this." We always work on projects together and were thrilled when we got our schedules during orientation and saw that we had three of our classes together: social studies, music, and science.

"Pick your groups, everyone. If you can't do it quietly, I will pick them for you. Then get to work on this introductory exercise." As she speaks, Mrs. Barton passes around sheets of paper.

"Who else do you want in our group?" I ask Soojin.

"We can ask Emily." Soojin points to where Emily is standing alone, scanning the room.

"*Emily?* Seriously?"

"Come on, Amina. She doesn't have a group, and we're not in elementary school anymore."

I'm stung by her words, but before I can even give in, Soojin has already waved Emily over.

"Do you want to be with us?" she offers. Emily is visibly relieved.

"Thanks, guys." Emily smiles at me, but I just manage to purse my lips together and nod. I don't understand. Doesn't Soojin remember all the crappy things that Emily has done for the past few years? Like the time she pinched her nose and squealed while Julie said something smelled like it had died when Soojin brought kimchee in her lunch. Or when they both scoffed at us and said, "Speak English, you're in America," while we were teaching each other phrases in Urdu and Korean. Or, worst of all, when she and Julie spread a rumor at school that Soojin's parents served dog meat at their downtown Milwaukee restaurant, Park Avenue Deli. Luke would bark under his breath every time he passed Soojin for months.

Why is Soojin acting like none of those things matter anymore?

"Oh good. You guys are a group of three? Here, Bradley, join these girls." Mrs. Barton thrusts Bradley Landry toward us. And this time, the three of us look at one another with alarm.

Bradley's the kid who can't sit still for more than five minutes. In second grade, he was forced to sit on a chair during circle time so he wouldn't start to roll around on the ground or poke the person next to him. And in fourth grade, he actually stuck his pen into the electrical socket while sitting on the carpet, got zapped, and was taken to the hospital in an ambulance.

"Sit with your groups for the next twenty minutes and come up with a strategy for the first exercise," Mrs. Barton calls out. I watch with dread as Bradley drags his chair over to my desk. Soojin and Emily bring theirs to form a rectangle.

"Let's do this." Bradley leans in too close to me, since he doesn't seem to understand personal space. I slide my chair away from him and start reading the handout, which describes our twenty-foot wagon and lists the supplies we can choose for our trip out West. Our first task is to pick items to stock the wagon with using the money we have. It's critical that we stay within the weight limit, or our oxen will be overtaxed.

"We definitely need sugar," Bradley starts. He holds the list close to his nose, slams it down on the table, and then points at the supply list.

"Sugar is a *luxury*," I protest. "We need flour more than sugar to survive."

"But I can't live without sugar." Bradley shakes his head. "Hey, do you guys have any candy in your desks?"

I shrug, but Emily speaks with authority. "No, Bradley, we don't. Why don't you make a list of the clothes you need to bring?"

At the end of the twenty minutes, after arguing for most of it, our group barely manages to complete our supply list. We let Bradley have some sugar in exchange for his agreeing to buy flour and a cast-iron pan. As time runs out, I scribble down the list, as exhausted as if I had actually loaded a wagon with hundreds of pounds of goods.

"Good job, everyone!" Mrs. Barton claps her hands. "We'll start our journeys on Monday."

"See ya, partners." Bradley slides his chair back to its usual spot, and I pack up.

When the final bell rings, I rush out of the room, ready to strategize with Soojin about how we are going to deal with this group and still win the race. Then someone calls out, "Wait up!"

Emily catches up to us, breathless. "That was fun. I think we have a good chance at winning," she says as she falls into step next to Soojin.

"Yeah, if Bradley doesn't get us all killed first," Soojin reminds her.

"It sucks we have to work with Bradley. He's *so* weird," Emily says. "Did you guys see what he was doing at lunch? He spread ice cream all over his pizza. It was so nasty!"

"Yeah," I mumble.

"And didn't he say all that weird stuff to your mom in second grade?" Emily continues.

"What did he say?" Soojin asks, turning to me. "You never told me."

"It was right before you moved here. In second grade my

mom came in and volunteered to do reading drills with one kid at a time. When it was Bradley's turn, he said, 'I'm going on a date with Amina's mom.'"

"Isn't that so weird?" Emily interrupts. "He rides my bus and is always getting in trouble." She keeps talking, so I don't get to finish the rest of my story—how Bradley also told Mama that he loved her and that he couldn't wait for their second date. Mama laughed and told Baba about what had happened with a funny little kid that night at dinner. But Baba immediately turned to me and said, "Stay away from that boy." Now I was stuck with Bradley every afternoon for as long as this project lasted: six whole weeks.

As Emily continues to speak, I trail behind them, listening to their conversation.

"Do you want to come over after school next week? We could work on our project or think of more names for you if you want."

"Yeah, sure. Maybe," Soojin answers when we reach her locker.

"Okay, great." Emily nods at me, looking puzzled. I

realize I'm staring at her blankly. "See you guys on Monday."

"Bye," Soojin replies as I wait for Emily to leave.

"Don't you think it's strange?" I finally say as she walks away. I'm embarrassed and feel petty, but I can't stop the words that are rattling around in my head from coming out.

"What do you mean?" Soojin asks.

"All of a sudden Emily is acting like she wants to be best friends with you or something."

"She's not so bad, Amina." Soojin puts on her new, mature middle-schooler voice. "Maybe you should give her a chance."

"What for?" I want to ask, but I don't have the nerve. Every time I say anything about Emily, I get the same feeling of disapproval from Soojin even though *I'm* not the one acting different. We've both felt the same way about Emily and Julie for so long. And I still feel the same.

Suddenly, I just want to get home as quickly as possible and start the weekend. I say a quick good-bye to Soojin and walk to my bus, turning my head to avoid Bradley as he rushes by to catch his. I catch a glimpse of a Blast from the

Past poster, and the huge words "Sign Up" underneath seem to scream out "YOU'RE A CHICKEN" to me. Everything about this past week—from wishing I were singing in the concert, to being in the worst pioneer wagon, to wondering why Soojin and Emily are acting so chummy—is making me wish I'd never left elementary school.

4

"It's our turn!" Rabiya shouts. She stomps her foot and thrusts out her hand for the game controller.

"We just started this game. Come back in half an hour." Yusuf doesn't take his eyes off the television or move from the best spot on the worn couch in their basement.

"Liar! You said that last time," Rabiya argues. Yusuf and Mustafa have been playing FIFA for more than an hour. So when they ignore her again, she throws her body in front of the TV and blocks the screen, shaking her hips from side to side.

"Move it," Yusuf growls as Mustafa pauses the game.

"Come on, Rabiya," Mustafa adds in a gentler tone.

"I'm winning. As soon as I finish crushing him, you guys can play."

Rabiya glares at them both, her big brown eyes blazing, and doesn't stop dancing. She's being a bit babyish for a ten-year-old, but I can't blame her. Her brother, Yusuf, is a year younger than Mustafa, even though he's taller, and always nasty to Rabiya. He actually makes Mustafa seem almost sweet in comparison.

"If I get up . . ." Yusuf pushes his glasses up his nose and waves his fist. His oversize jersey and baggy jeans make him seem even bigger than usual, and Rabiya looks like a tiny bird hopping around in front of a beast that can easily crush her.

"Forget it," I interrupt. "I don't even want to play anymore. Let's just go upstairs." We were waiting to put on the new version of Just Dance, but I'm not very good at it anyway. Soojin gets four stars on every song when she and I play together, but she's been studying ballet, tap, and jazz since she was six. And Rabiya spends way too much time practicing. I know that my feet only work to help me keep time when I sing and press the pedals on the piano. I'm a klutz when it comes to dancing.

"I'm telling on you guys," Rabiya finally threatens. The boys don't respond. They know that our parents are sipping chai with plates of tea biscuits upstairs and that they aren't the slightest bit interested in our bickering.

I follow Rabiya upstairs, trying not to trip over the deep-pink shalwar kameez Mama forced me to wear. Rabiya's mom, Salma Auntie, brought it back from a visit to Pakistan, and Mama wanted to make sure she saw me in it before it gets too small for me. The embroidery on the neckline is so itchy that I'm tempted to change into the pajamas I brought along in case I spend the night.

"Let's ask about the sleepover again," Rabiya whispers when we get to the top of the stairs. "Maybe they'll feel bad the boys are being mean to us and let you stay."

"Okay," I agree, although Salma Auntie already refused during dinner. She complained that we always stay up too late talking and are tardy for Sunday school. And since she is running the book fair at the Islamic Center, she didn't want to miss anything tomorrow. I, on the other hand, am always more than happy to miss as much of Sunday school as possible.

Our parents are engrossed in conversation while the television blares in the background. A fast-paced Indian song pulses as Bollywood actresses in crimson outfits twirl in perfect coordination in front of a stage decorated with yellow and red flowers. I love the sound of the drums mixed with the strings, although the super-high-pitched, tinny singing grates on my ears.

"Why are you worried about your brother's visit?" Salma Auntie is asking Baba as we creep into the room and stand behind the sofa.

"You know there's some bad feeling in this country toward Muslims, and all this negative news these days."

"But he must read the news and know this already," Hamid Uncle argues. "It shouldn't be a shock to him."

"Maybe. But what if someone says something to him? He wears a kufi and has a long beard."

"Nothing like that will happen here. We have a strong

community, and there are so many Muslims living in Milwaukee. People have been good to us," Mama says.

"Yes, but Bhai Jaan is also so set in his ways. I'm just nervous he won't like it here."

"Let's go upstairs," Rabiya whispers. "This is boring."

I shake my head. I want to keep listening to find out what Baba thinks my uncle won't like about America.

Is he afraid he won't like me?

"Come on!" Rabiya hisses, and tugs my hand.

"What are you two doing here? This is adult talk. Go upstairs," Salma Auntie scolds as she peers behind the sofa at us. We look at each other and shrug and then follow orders and go upstairs. It isn't the right time to ask about sleepovers.

As we pass Yusuf's bedroom, Rabiya darts inside and grabs a fistful of gum balls from his old-fashioned machine. Then we sprawl on Rabiya's bedspread, blowing bubbles and doing our favorite thing: watching YouTube videos that ordinary people posted of themselves doing crazy stunts. One guy makes a basketball shot from a thousand miles away. It hits the roof of a house, bounces off a tree, and swishes into a hoop.

"That can't be real," Rabiya insists. "It's camera tricks for sure."

I make a mental note to show Mustafa later. He'll be impressed, camera tricks or not.

"Look at this one. This girl is just singing a Taylor Swift song into a webcam. She has six thousand views, and she isn't even *good*," Rabiya scoffs.

I can't help but agree. The girl is singing a cappella and is totally off tempo.

"Let's make our own video! You sing, and I'll do backup. It'll be way better than this one." Rabiya starts to look through her song library.

"A video? No way. What if someone clicks on it?" I ask. Rabiya and I have basically grown up like sisters so, like Soojin, she knows I can sing.

"That's the point, genius!" Rabiya laughs. "What's the use having an amazing voice if no one ever hears it?"

"My parents hear it."

"Yeah. Exactly. What if Taylor Swift had been too scared to ever sing in front of other people? Or Adele?"

"I'm no Adele," I object.

"Fine. No one is Adele. But you are an awesome singer, Amina. Come on. What do you want to sing?"

"Nothing."

"Come on. It's just for practice. I'm not posting it or anything. And if you don't get up, I'm recording you like that, sitting there in your fancy shalwar kameez!" Rabiya threatens me with the same fierce eyes she used on Yusuf downstairs. It makes me smile. I think of the concert and how I haven't told her about passing on the chance to sing a solo. She would push and push and probably show up at my school and sign my name on the sheet for me. And for a second I wish she went to the same school as me instead of living fifteen minutes away in Bay View, in a quiet tree-lined neighborhood almost identical to ours.

We spend the next hour in front of the webcam trying to record ourselves singing an Avril Lavigne song Rabiya picked out. But we keep messing up, either because we stumble over the words or start cracking up.

"Start it over!" Rabiya falls out of the camera's view.

"I need some water." I'm getting hoarse from singing and laughing so hard. But then I hear my mom calling my name to meet everyone at the bottom of the stairs.

"Next time I'll destroy you," Yusuf declares as he and Mustafa emerge from the basement. Mustafa yelps as he is wrestled into a headlock.

"Khuda hafiz, beti," Salma Auntie says to me. She hands me leftover rice packed into an empty yogurt container to carry home.

I remember to duck in time before Hamid Uncle pinches my cheek, and repeat the words of farewell.

"Khuda hafiz, Auntie and Uncle. Thank you for having us."

My parents keep talking to their friends for another ten minutes while I stand in the entryway, burning up in my jacket. All of us kids bug our eyes and moan. It's the same thing every single time.

"We could have played another game," Yusuf grumbles

43

to Mustafa. Rabiya starts to nod off, sitting on the stairs. But then just as I'm about to give up and join her, we walk out and pile into the car. An Adele song comes on the radio, and as I imagine myself in a video hitting every note as well as her, I drift to sleep.

5

The swarm of kids pours into a small courtyard, where a volunteer hands out slices of lukewarm pizza from a box. It's the break between classes during Sunday school, and I'm starving even though it's only eleven a.m.

"Take a drink." The lady motions to me. I grab my paper plate and can of lemonade and hurry to a bench where Rabiya and our friend Dahlia are eating their pizza. Their class always gets out earlier than mine, and they are a level ahead of me. In Sunday school, your age or grade in regular school doesn't matter. It all depends on how well you can connect Arabic letters into words and how many passages from the Quran, or surahs, you can recite from memory.

"Hey, that's a pretty one," I say to Dahlia, pointing to the blue zigzag-patterned scarf expertly wrapped around her head. My own slid off my head as I walked toward them and is hanging around my neck like a miniature cape.

"Thanks," Dahlia says. She carefully bites up to the crust of her pizza. "This one's my mom's." Dahlia always wears the hijab, and not just at the Islamic Center. She even sports it at the middle school she goes to. I can't imagine what it would be like to walk through Greendale Middle School and be the only person with a scarf on, but Dahlia makes it seem as natural as wearing a headband, no matter where she is.

"Imam Malik subbed for our class today," Rabiya says. "And it was so much fun."

"Lucky!" I reply. I take a couple of bites of the pizza, but the oily cheese makes me want to gag, so I stop. "Sister Naima spent half of our class making everyone take turns reading the same line of the Quran over and over again."

"Boring," they both chime in unison.

"And she kept yelling the same thing: 'You're saying it wrong. Not the little *haa*, the big *haa*!'"

"Well, that's because Sister Naima is from Egypt, like my family," Dahlia says.

"So?" Rabiya asks.

"So her Arabic is perfect."

"Well, Imam Malik isn't from Egypt, and his Arabic is awesome," Rabiya argues.

I agree. Imam Malik grew up in Florida and can easily switch between perfect Arabic and English. Even better, he knows as much about cheat codes to video games as religious topics.

"Yeah, but his parents are Arab," Dahlia reminds us. "No offense, but people from Pakistan don't really know how to pronounce Arabic the right way."

I'm not offended. Dahlia is right about how most Pakistani people, including my parents, pronounce Arabic differently. I just can't make certain sounds in the Arabic alphabet. No matter how perfect my musical pitch is, it just doesn't translate to Arabic. Plus, my brain doesn't register the way the letters change when they connect to one another, and I get them wrong all the time. I always feel embarrassed when it's my turn to read aloud to the class, and that's the biggest reason I don't like Sunday school.

"We'd better go back inside." Rabiya points to the crowd moving back into the community building that holds the classrooms and social hall. It looks like a giant shoe box next to the shiny curved dome of the mosque with two towering minarets. I climb the narrow stairway back to my classroom, trying to avoid getting jostled.

The second hour of Sunday school is when I can relax while Sister Naima tells stories of the prophets. Today is one of my favorite stories: the one of Prophet Yusuf and his jealous brothers who threw him into a well. Sister Naima gets super animated as she explains the events and waves her arms around as if she's acting them out. "Jealousy is a terrible thing," she warns, and I feel ashamed as Emily pops into my head.

Am I jealous of her? Or is it okay if I just want her to go back to her old friends?

"Don't forget to do your homework!" Sister Naima shouts as class ends and everyone rushes out. I head to the mosque for prayer, stopping first at the bathroom to do wudu. There's a special faucet at knee height with a little bench in front, where I sit and rub my hands in the cold water before rinsing my mouth and nose. I splash my face and hairline and pass a wet hand over my ears and neck. Then I roll up my sleeves and wash up to the elbow before finally kicking off my sandals and running my feet through the stream of water.

I walk out, shaking off the extra water, and adjust my scarf tight around my head so it won't fall off again. I enter the cool mosque, slip off my sandals on the marble floor by the women's entrance, and put them neatly onto the shelves.

Rabiya has saved me a spot on the plush green carpet next to her. In the hush of the prayer hall, with its crystal chandelier, gold trim, and big plaques with Arabic calligraphy decorating the walls, a familiar calm washes over me. A woman in front of us kneels in prayer, touching her head to the ground while her baby tugs on her shirt. An older lady mouths prayers with a string of beads in her hand. And I spot Mama in the corner reading the Quran quietly with Salma Auntie and their other friends.

My earliest memory of the mosque is being here with my parents during Ramadan for special nightly prayers when I was three or four. I stood with Mama in my tiny headscarf with sewn-in elastic to keep it in place and tried to stay still. But after a while, I'd get bored and wander to the back of the prayer hall and run around with the other kids while different ladies took turns hushing us.

Imam Malik's voice comes over the speakers. "Brothers and sisters, I have a few announcements. First, the book sale will be going on for one hour after prayer in the community hall. Second, we are taking nominations for PTA officers. And finally, I'm excited to share that we will be hosting our first Quran recitation competition for students from all over the state on November fifteenth, insha'Allah."

A few people start murmuring as the imam continues.

"All students are encouraged to participate. I'm sure you'll make us proud. The winner will get four tickets to Six Flags and a big check for college savings."

The buzz grows louder.

"We'll be handing out a flyer next Sunday, but, parents,

make sure to register your kids as soon as possible."

Uh-oh! I turn my head back toward Mama to see if she is paying attention, but she is still looking at the Quran. I think back to my moment of panic when my voice left me stranded during the second-grade play. If I couldn't manage to speak English, which I'm *fluent* in, on a stage, how would I possibly make out Arabic words in my pathetic accent? This Quran competition is something I want nothing to do with. I say a quick prayer that Mama wasn't paying attention and that she won't sign me up as everyone gets up and stands in neat rows. Folding my hands across my chest, I try to concentrate as the imam starts to lead us in prayer with the familiar praise of God, "Bismillāhi r-raḥmāni r-raḥīm . . ."

6

"Are you kidding me?" Baba shouts. "That's pass interference! Where's the call?"

"That's good defense," Mustafa counters. A little smirk plays on his lips.

"Get your eyes checked!" Baba scowls at the black-and-white-striped referee on the television screen, shaking his head while Mustafa snickers.

"You too," Baba glowers. "You and your Packers. Bunch of cheaters!"

"Why do you care so much? You're not playing in the game, are you?" Mama says from the corner of the room where she's dumped out a mound of laundry. She sits folding clothes into neat piles on the carpet.

"Yeah, Baba, chill out. Your Bears are only down by thirteen." Mustafa pats Baba on the leg.

"I'll chill you out." Baba pushes Mustafa over on the sofa and starts pounding him on the shoulder, while Mama laughs and throws balled socks at them.

I watch the commotion, safe in my favorite leather armchair, where I'm curled up with a worn copy of *Life on the Oregon Trail.* I checked out the fat volume from the school library in the hopes it would help give our team an advantage in Mrs. Barton's social studies project. The book is filled with diary entries written by the pioneers themselves during their time on the trail, and even though a lot of it is flat-out horrifying, I can't stop reading it. I shudder thinking of the kids my age who walked fifteen miles a day for months, carrying everything they owned with them in their wagons, only to get an awful disease and be buried in shallow graves along the trail or drown in a river crossing. It suddenly makes working with my wagon group seem like a trip to the mall.

"Aren't you tired yet? Three hours of watching these helmets just jumping on each other," Mama asks.

I already sorted my clothes and took them upstairs to my room. Then I practiced singing one of the solo choices Ms. Holly had listed for the winter concert—just for fun. It was "A Change Is Gonna Come," performed by Aretha Franklin.

It felt incredibly satisfying to blast out the words "I was born by the river . . ." in my biggest voice. Something about the song made me feel powerful, and I even started to daydream about signing up for the concert and finally getting the chance to surprise everyone with my secret. Just like Stella on *The Voice*, I could transform from a skinny, shy girl in a plaid shirt and jeans into a glamorous star in a sequined gown. Well, maybe I'd skip the sequined-gown part, but I could at least be confident, sure-of-herself Amina—ready to share my talent with the school, and, eventually, with the rest of the world.

But then I remembered how my voice would betray me, shrink back, and cling to my lungs, while I stupidly stand on a stage with people staring at me. I turned off the song and went back downstairs.

"It's over," Baba says. "Two minutes. They can't come back." He flips off the TV and shakes his head.

"Okay, then—get up, everyone. I need your help." Mama picks up her notepad, where she always scribbles down important to-do lists. I dread that notepad. "Thaya Jaan is coming in less than two weeks, and we need to get this house ready."

"Right now?" Mustafa complains. "I think I have English homework to finish."

"Oh, *now* you remember your homework after sitting on that sofa all day? No, get up," Mama commands. "You will have plenty of time after dinner."

"What do you want us to do?" Baba asks tentatively.

"I need you to take this laundry upstairs, then go through that pile in the corner of the garage. Mustafa, I want you to dust all the lights and ceiling fans using the ladder and put away that extra bedding in the guest room."

"What about Amina?" Mustafa points to where I'm

sitting with my book in front of my face, hoping Mama won't notice me.

"I'm getting to her. Amina, take out the good cutlery and polish the silver serving dishes."

"Jaani," Baba starts, using his affectionate name for Mama. "Believe me; Bhai Jaan doesn't care about polished silver or what we keep in the garage. Besides, garages are meant for junk."

Mustafa and I exchange hopeful looks. Maybe Baba can convince Mama to relax and forget the chores.

"No, your brother is used to a big house with lots of help, where everything is perfect. And you are all the help I have. Now get up!" Mama clearly means business, so we all get moving.

I rummage through the china cabinet in the dining room and pull out green boxes of silver serving spoons blackened with tarnish. Polishing silver reminds me of preschool, where I did all these random chores like sorting, scrubbing, and sewing giant buttons with a blunt needle. I actually kind of still like it. I sit down at the kitchen table and hum while I smear the thick pink polish all over the spoons with a cotton ball and watch it pull off the layer of black.

Mama is a blur of activity as she minces a huge pile of onions and garlic in a mini chopper and puts a jumbo pot on the stove. When the onions are sizzling in the pot, Mama throws in fresh ginger, tomatoes, and spices to create the masala that forms the base of all her meals. Even with the window open and the kitchen exhaust fan running, the house will soon be filled with the scent. I've already made sure that my bedroom door is shut tight so my clothes won't absorb the smell. And luckily I'm not going anywhere else today, since it's probably already penetrated my hair.

I learned my lesson about the cooking smell the hard way after I left my hoodie in the kitchen one morning in fourth grade while Mama was up early cooking before work. When I got to the elementary school's all-purpose room to wait for the first morning bell, Julie took a big, exaggerated sniff from across the room and asked, "Did somebody bring in Chinese food?" Then, like a bloodhound working a trail, she made her way over to me, where she finally said in her most offended tone, "Oh my God. It's *you*."

Everyone started to laugh. And then Luke, always the most obnoxious kid in the class, started calling me "Hunan Express," which Emily thought was hilarious and kept repeating over and over again. Even though the nickname didn't stick, I was humiliated for at least three days, until Luke forgot about me and moved on to his next victim. My face burns with the memory as my eyes sting from the spices.

"What are you making?" I ask Mama, trying not to think about Emily or why Soojin is acting like she is okay with her all of a sudden. The big pots are usually reserved for dinner parties, and Mama hasn't mentioned having one any time soon.

"I'm making food to freeze for when Thaya Jaan comes."

"Really? Why don't you just cook when he's here?" I ask. "How much extra is one man going to eat?"

"I don't want to serve him leftovers. I'm going to freeze this for the days I don't have time to cook."

Baba walks in from the garage, holding a dust-covered mini vacuum.

"Do you want this?" he asks Mama.

"No, it doesn't work. Just throw it away." Mama waves her hand. "How do we collect so much rubbish?"

"Is someone coming over for dinner?" Baba asks, peering into the pots on the stove.

"No!" Mama grumbles. "I'm cooking for your brother."

Baba laughs. "I told you already, don't overdo it. . . ."

Mama, beads of sweat covering her forehead, lets out a long sigh. "First you talk about how Bhai Jaan is like a father to you and how you are worried he won't be happy here. And now you tell me *not* to get ready for him?"

"I'm not worried that he won't like the food or how clean the house is. I'm worried he won't like the way things are here or the way we live!"

What's wrong with the way we live?

I stop polishing and freeze in my seat, hoping my parents won't make me leave the room like they usually do when they have an argument.

"There's nothing wrong with the way we live." Mama stirs the food in the pot hard, and her spoon hits the sides.

"We work hard and have raised good, decent children."

"I know, I know. But Bhai Jaan is so . . . traditional. He worries about us turning away from Islam. And you know everything to him is black and white." Baba speaks in a hush, as if his brother might overhear him from thousands of miles away.

"Do you think he won't want us to go trick-or-treating?" I interrupt without thinking.

Baba turns around, startled to see me. "What do you mean, geeta?" His voice is suddenly soft.

"Well, remember last year at Sunday school, a few of the parents and teachers were saying that trick-or-treating was haram? That Halloween came from devil worshipping or something, and that we shouldn't do it?"

Baba frowns, even though his eyes look amused. "I don't know if Thaya Jaan has ever heard of Halloween or trick-or-treating, but I'm guessing he wouldn't like it much."

"If he's here on Halloween, can we still go?" Soojin and I already decided that we're going to dress up together, as ketchup and mustard bottles.

"Yes, yes, of course you can go." Now it's Baba's turn to sigh. He looks at Mama, who sits down with a glass of water across from me.

"You're right, jaani," he says to Mama. "We're both worried about Bhai Jaan's visit for different reasons. But it will be fine."

"I hope so," Mama says. But she sounds totally unconvinced.

"And besides," Baba continues as Mustafa walks into the kitchen, "my brother memorized the Quran when we were young and hasn't forgotten a letter. He can help the kids prepare for the competition."

"What competition?" Mustafa asks. He grabs an apple from the fruit bowl and tears a chunk out of it with his teeth.

"Didn't you hear Imam Malik talk about it before prayer?"

"Oh, um, I must have been concentrating on prayer," Mustafa says quickly between chews. "I didn't hear him." He looks at the ground as he speaks.

"Well, the center is hosting a statewide Quran competition for the students, and I signed you both up."

"You did *what*?" Mustafa spits out the words. "I'm not doing it!"

"Mustafa, watch your mouth," Mama warns.

"Shouldn't I have a say in this?" Mustafa asks, looking back and forth at Mama and Baba with raised eyebrows.

My stomach starts to churn, and not from the food smells or because I'm getting hungry for dinner. It's a mixture of hating to see Mustafa argue with our parents and dreading the idea of the competition.

But maybe Mustafa can get us both out of it.

"Imam Malik specifically asked that you and Amina participate. He wants our support, and we should give it to him." Baba isn't about to take a request from the imam lightly. Even though there's a big age difference between them, he's a good friend of Baba's, and he used to visit us often before he got married last year. He even taught Mustafa how to ice-skate when he was little.

"You know I have school? And homework? This is going to take up a lot of my time," Mustafa argues.

"You make time for basketball," Baba warns. "You will

make time for this, too." Since Mustafa got the permission he needed to try out and made the team, he's been extra good about getting his homework done and taking out the trash and recycling without being nagged. He's also stopped talking back as often as usual. Until right now.

"Aw, come on! I don't want to stand up and recite Arabic in front of a bunch of random people. I'm not that good at it, and it's just . . . *awkward*."

Amen, brother.

"Not *people*, Mustafa. This is your community," Mama corrects. "It's just as important as your team or your friends. You are an example for the younger kids."

"So basically you're saying I have no choice?" Mustafa waves his half-eaten apple in exasperation.

"Yes, we are saying that," Baba says firmly.

Mustafa stares at him and opens his mouth to say something else. But instead, he takes another big bite of his apple, turns, and leaves the kitchen.

I don't dare say a word. My parents are clearly united on this and convinced that the competition is something their kids have to do. There's no point trying to tell them that speaking in front of a crowd is something I haven't gotten over, as much as everyone tells me I need to, or warning them that my Arabic performance is just going to embarrass them anyway. Baba would just say his piece about "What's this embarrassing?" and "Why do you care what other people think?" I wouldn't dare point out that he cares a whole lot what Thaya Jaan and Imam Malik think. Plus, at this point, they would just think I was making excuses like Mustafa. I bite my nails, deep in thought.

One way or another, I'm going to find some way to get out of the competition.

7

Soojin turns the key in the front door of her house and pushes it open, setting off a loud beeping.

"Hold on a sec." She runs to punch a code into the alarm panel. "Come on in. Mom's got class this afternoon, and Grandpa's probably asleep upstairs."

I pull off my sneakers and line them up on the small carpet near the front door. Soojin's house always reminds me of mine. No one wears shoes indoors, and there's always the faint scent of food lingering in the air.

"I'm so hungry," Soojin moans. She drops her backpack with a thud at the foot of the stairs and hurries into the kitchen.

I follow her after leaving my book bag by the door, and Soojin is already inside the pantry. "What do you want? Chips? Rice crackers? Oreos?"

"Chips sound good. Can I get a drink?" I make sure to open the refrigerator near the sink. The first time I visited Soojin after school, I hadn't realized that there were two refrigerators in the kitchen. The extra fridge is reserved for making kimchi, fermented vegetables that sit in there for weeks. I pulled open the door without any warning, got a big whiff of the overwhelming pickled odor, and yelled, "AAH!" Soojin and Mrs. Park laughed as I slammed the door shut.

After pouring two glasses of apple juice, I sit next to Soojin on a barstool, and we munch on cheese-flavored chips. Actually, I munch while she inhales hers and then waits for me to finish.

"Where's Kyung Mi?" I ask. Soojin's sister, a fourth grader, reminds me of a mini, shyer, and quieter version of Soojin and often makes me wish I had a real little sister—in addition to Rabiya. But Soojin finds her annoying.

"She has art class."

"How come you don't take art classes anymore?" Soojin used to be into making crafts, and I still have the handmade block-print birthday card she made me last year.

"I like dancing more." Soojin has jazz and ballet classes twice a week after school, and any chance she has she leaps down the empty hallways at school.

I hear a floorboard squeak and see an older man in a brown cardigan shuffling into the room with his arms held behind his back. Soojin quickly stands up and bows deeply.

"An-yŏng-ha-se-yo," she greets her grandfather.

I stand up and bow too. Soojin's grandfather doesn't speak much English, but like always, he smiles warmly and bends slightly in return.

Over the years Soojin has taught me enough phrases of Korean that I understand when Soojin asks her grandfather if he wants her to get him anything to eat. He shakes his head, makes himself some tea, and cuts up a pear in precise quarters before shuffling into the family room. There he settles into an armchair and flips on a Korean satellite channel with the volume turned up extra loud.

"Let's go to my room," Soojin says. "We won't be able to hear anything in here." The overdramatic music that accompanies the show sounds like the mind-numbing background tracks of the Urdu dramas that my parents watch at home, so I'm glad to leave.

I always like hanging out in Soojin's room, which is smaller than mine and painted a pretty green. Two prints in red frames hang over the bed, each with one bold black Korean letter. The first time I came over I asked Soojin what the letters meant, and she explained that they spelled her name, which meant "treasure." Since I thought that was so cool, I'd given her a silver necklace with a little treasure-chest charm for her tenth birthday. Soojin has worn it every day since, but now I wonder how it will all be different when she changes her name.

Will she still wear my necklace? Will she take down those frames and decorate with a tacky mug that says Melanie on it?

"They're saying that this is going to be the snowiest winter we've had in decades," I say. "I hope we get lots of snow days."

"Me too. We didn't get any last year."

I live for snow days. We have to get at least a foot in Milwaukee, but when things do shut down, it's like a block party. We have epic snowball fights, Mama and I go cross-country skiing, and Mustafa makes tons of money shoveling driveways.

"We didn't get any science or math homework today," I say.

"Yeah, but Mrs. Barton said we have to read up for our next wagon trail assignment."

"I have been. Do you know the pioneers used to eat squirrels?"

"Gross. Except I can see Bradley being into that!" Soojin flops on top of her bed. "Although, did you notice that he actually has some good ideas?"

"I know. He was totally right about how to cross the river. I think he's a Boy Scout or something in real life."

"And Emily's been pretty good too," Soojin says.

"What do you mean?"

"I mean she's a good partner and is helping us win."

I pause, trying to convince myself not to say anything. "So do you . . . like *want* to be *friends* with her now?" It just comes out.

"I don't know. She used to be really immature. But I think she's changed. She's making an effort, and she's not so bad."

Not so bad? I chew on my lip, afraid to say anything else. Emily has made me so angry—and been obnoxious to Soojin and me—for so long. And now Soojin seems to be forgetting so easily.

"Are you, um, going to go to her house this week?" I stare down at my book so she can't see my face.

"I don't know. I forgot to ask my mom."

I exhale slowly. Soojin isn't rushing to spend extra time with Emily. But I can't help wishing again, no matter how much better it has been than I expected, that I had suggested someone else to join our group first. That way I wouldn't have to feel like a bad person for being unwelcoming. And like the Oregon Trail, I wouldn't have to pioneer the uncharted territory of Soojin finding Emily "not so bad."

8

"We got it!" Soojin shouts two days later, rushing into the gym, where the rest of us are waiting for the morning bell to ring. Her face is flushed with excitement.

"Got what?" I ask.

"Our date for our swearing-in. It's official—I'm going to be a citizen!" Soojin does a little leap of joy.

"That's great!" I say as some of the other kids came over to find out what the commotion is about.

"My dad is so excited. Yesterday afternoon he bought us all these." Soojin points to a little American flag pin on her sweatshirt.

I can imagine Baba doing something like that too. But

my parents became citizens when I was much younger, so I don't remember it.

"When is it? What do you have to do?" Margot asks.

"October twentieth—just two weeks! Hundreds of people will be there, and I think we all pledge allegiance to the flag together. I get to miss school and everything."

"Lucky!" Allison says.

"That's really cool," I say.

As the bell rings and everyone starts filing out to class, Soojin grabs my arm.

"And . . . I've decided on my new name!" she whispers in my ear.

"What is it? Melanie?" I try to act like it's no big deal.

"Susan." Soojin looks at me expectantly.

"Susan?"

"Yeah, what do you think?"

"That's not one of the names you liked before, is it?"

"I know. I just thought of it last night. It's pretty close to Soojin, right?" Soojin grins.

"Yeah. But then . . . why don't you just stay Soojin?"

I wish I could take the words back as Soojin's expression instantly sours.

"I thought you would get it by now," she complains.

"I do, I do," I agree. "Susan is a really nice name." My eyes fall on the treasure chest charm hanging around Soojin's neck.

"Thanks." Soojin squeezes my arm. "I think so too."

"Hi, guys!" Emily calls out as we pass her in the hall.

We aren't guys.

Soojin goes over to talk with Emily at her locker, and, as I keep walking down the hall, I hear them discussing the swearing-in. An uneasy feeling settles over me that lasts throughout the day, and bubbles up inside me again during social studies. I'm sitting next to Bradley and trying to concentrate on our assignment, which is hard enough. But as I watch the girls chatting out of the corner of my eye and see Emily lean in and say something to Soojin that makes her smile, a spark of unmistakable jealousy shoots through my chest.

Then, to make matters worse, Bradley delivers unexpected challenges to our westward journey.

"Amina has cholera. And our wagon lost a wheel."

9

"I see him!" Baba strains his neck to peer through the security exit at the arrivals terminal of Chicago O'Hare International Airport.

A stout Latino man in a black sport coat trudges through the automatic sliding doors.

I giggle, but Baba ignores me. He's so nervous about his brother's arrival that he's been pacing the hall and jumping whenever he spots someone with a tan complexion or a white beard. He made us leave four hours early and drove us the hour and a half to Chicago way before Thaya Jaan's flight was due to arrive.

"Why isn't he out yet? The plane landed an hour ago,"

Baba repeats for the fifth time as he runs his hand through his hair like he does whenever he's anxious.

"He will be here soon," Mama says. She's carefully resting on an airport chair, trying not to wrinkle her fancy maroon-and-black shalwar kameez.

"What if Immigration is giving him a hard time? Or maybe they are going through his bags in Customs?" Baba asks.

"It'll be fine. Don't worry," Mama says.

I can't remember the last time I've seen Baba this jumpy. He's wearing his navy tweed blazer and shiny, polished shoes. At Mama's insistence, I'm in a velvet party dress, and even Mustafa grudgingly agreed to put on an ironed shirt and some jeans without any holes. Waiting together, we look like the families I see at the mall posing with Santa, dressed in their holiday best, even though it's only the first week of October.

"There he is!" Baba points as the doors open. Thaya Jaan emerges in a rumpled shirt, a white kufi pressed over his thick gray-and-white hair.

Baba rushes toward him, and the two brothers thump each other on the back and smile. Then Mama steps forward and bows her head slightly in front of her brother-in-law.

"Assalaamwalaikum, Bhai Jaan. We're so happy you came," she says.

I stand back, uncertain whether I'm supposed to hug my uncle or wait for him to pat me on the head, like the older uncles in the community always do.

"Amina, Mustafa." Baba motions us closer as if we're strangers needing a formal introduction.

"My sweet Amina," Thaya Jaan says as he plants a big kiss on my forehead. He throws his arm around Mustafa and kisses him on the cheek too, which Mustafa wipes off a second later.

"What a big boy you are, Mustafa. I'm so happy to be seeing my niece and nephew after so long." His voice is deep and gruffer than on the telephone, and he speaks slowly in Urdu. I respond with the few polite phrases that my parents have taught me to say to uncles and aunties. But after all the usual things, I run out of things to say. Luckily, Baba carries the conversation.

"Let me help you." He grabs a rolling suitcase from Thaya Jaan while Mustafa takes his briefcase. I sneak peeks at my uncle, who is slightly taller than Baba and looks a lot more like him in real life than in pictures. They have the same thick eyebrows and strong, straight noses. The main difference is that Baba still has a lot of dark hair, while Thaya Jaan's is mostly white. His matching white beard is thick and long, which also makes me think of Santa again.

"How was your trip? Were you able to sleep? You must be hungry?" Baba fires off questions as we walk toward baggage claim to get the rest of the luggage.

"It was a long journey, but I'm here now, Alhamdulillah."

"Yes, Alhamdulillah," Baba repeats enthusiastically.

Thaya Jaan turns his head, taking in the row of retail shops selling cheap souvenirs, fast food, magazines, and candy. Crowds of travelers, airport staff, and flight crews rush by us in both directions. I wonder what he thinks of

America so far and hope he likes what he sees, but his eyes are hard to read.

"Walk faster, Amina," Mama says. "Let's hurry up and get Thaya Jaan home. We have a long drive."

"Come, my dear." Thaya Jaan puts his arm around me. I smile up at him. *Maybe I was nervous for no reason.*

10

"Please, take some more, Bhai Jaan. You've hardly eaten." Mama picks up a silver serving dish that I polished the week before, now filled with spicy spinach-and-lamb stew, and holds it out in front of Thaya Jaan.

My plate is still half-full. Even though I only took a little bit of everything, it ends up being way too much food for me to eat. Not only is there stew, but also curried chicken, lentils, rice with vegetables, naan, salad, and yogurt sauce. The spread looks like what Mama puts out for a full-fledged dinner party, even though the guests are missing. And instead of being stuck eating with the kids in the kitchen or in the basement, Mustafa and I are actually sitting at the dining room table, eating off the gold-rimmed china, and wiping our chins with stiff, starched white cloth napkins.

Thaya Jaan waves away the dish and shakes his head.

"No more. Everything was delicious. But I can't eat another bite." Mama spoons more curry onto his plate despite his protests.

"Amina, go put water on for chai, please," she says. "Mustafa, please clear the table."

Luckily, she's too distracted to notice how much food I have left or to say anything about it, so I take my plate with me. Mustafa stacks a few more and follows me into the kitchen.

"That was a ridiculous amount of food." He shakes his head as he places the plates in the sink. "Ma can't keep this up for three months."

"I know. Did you see all those leftovers?"

"Let's get Thaya Jaan to say he wants nothing but burgers, pizza, and chicken wings from now on."

"And that he wants to eat on paper plates." I eye the growing pile of dishes with dread.

I fill the heavy silver kettle with water and take out the worn mugs we normally use, before thinking twice and pulling out the matching gold-rimmed teacups and saucers.

"What's for dessert?" Mustafa peers into the refrigerator. "Oh yes!" He carefully lifts out a crystal bowl filled with round balls floating in a thick honey-colored syrup.

"Gulab jamun? When did Mama make those?" I wonder. The sticky, sweet, doughnutlike treats are my favorite Pakistani dessert but take hours to prepare.

Mama comes in, carrying two platters of food from the dining table.

"Can you both clear the rest of the table and load the dishwasher?" She lets out a tired yawn. Mustafa mouths the word "pizza" to me, and I grin back at him, feeling like my old brother is back for a minute.

When the tea is ready, we gather around Thaya Jaan in the family room. Mama fixes a cup for Thaya Jaan, mixing sugar into the steaming milky brew scented with cardamom. I bite into my gulab jamun and am instantly hit by a jolt of sweetness.

"So, Bhai Jaan, tell us. How are things in Pakistan?" Baba asks as he places his empty glass dessert bowl on the coffee table with a satisfied expression.

"It's getting more and more difficult each day." Thaya Jaan's eyes look sad. "Things are getting so expensive—even basics like flour cost so much that it's hard for poor people to afford simple bread. May Allah have mercy on them."

My gulab jamun turns into a lead ball in my gut as I think of the uneaten food on my plate that I just scraped into the garbage.

"But our family is doing well, Alhamdulillah," Thaya Jaan continues. "The business is growing, and the kids are fine. Ahmed was admitted to medical school."

"Wonderful!" Baba says. "You must be so proud of him."

Mustafa studies his fingernails closely.

"Everybody was sending you all their love, and, how can I forget? Mustafa, bring me my suitcase, please. Your cousins sent a few things."

Mustafa jumps up to get the suitcase and drags it over. Thaya Jaan unzips it and pulls out a pile of oddly shaped packages. I think of Santa Thaya again as he distributes the presents.

"This is for you, Amina, from your Thayee Jaan." He passes me a lumpy gift wrapped in crinkly pink cellophane. "And these are from your cousins."

The crinkly paper holds a bright blue shalwar kameez with a tiny purple paisley pattern and gold buttons. I also unwrap delicate bangles made out of glass, covered in newspaper with Urdu lettering on it. One of my cousins sent me a small lacquered jewelry box. Another gave me a blue-and-white-beaded wall hanging with a big Arabic "Allah" carved out of wood dangling from it.

"This wasn't necessary, Bhai Jaan. Everyone's love and prayers are enough." Baba seems embarrassed as he touches the collar of the new black shalwar kameez his brother handed him.

"Nonsense. It is just tokens. Everyone misses you and wants you to visit."

That's true, at least according to the handwritten note on tissue-thin paper that came with my gifts.

My dearest Amina. I trust you are well. What class are you in now? When will you visit us? It has been a long time. I hope you like these bangles and they fit you. And one day I hope we see each other soon. Please come to Pakistan. Khuda hafiz, Maryam.

I haven't seen my cousins in six years and hardly remember them apart from a few memories of playing dolls with the girls and stealing mangos and dried dates from the kitchen when the cook wasn't looking. My cousins are people I don't really think of until I get an occasional photo or formal letters like this. I wish I knew them better.

"When will you all come to visit Pakistan?" Thaya Jaan asks, as if he's reading my mind. "It has been too long."

"Soon, Bhai Jaan, we will visit, insha'Allah," Baba says. He always says insha'Allah when he talks about the future since it means "God willing." "We have been talking about it, but it is hard."

That's true too. I often hear my parents talk about visiting Pakistan as a family again, but then they add that it isn't the right time to be away from work, or that we shouldn't miss school. And lately, we hear more and more frightening stories of people from America getting sick or robbed while visiting. The discussions usually end with "maybe we'll go next year, when things are better, insha'Allah."

"Your children need to know where they come from." Thaya Jaan's forehead wrinkles, and he frowns. "And why don't they speak Urdu?"

Baba shifts in his seat.

"They understand it, but we speak both English and Urdu to them, and the kids respond to us in English," he says. *Baba seems ashamed of us.* I suddenly wish Urdu didn't jumble in my head and come out all wrong. It's just as bad as when I try to read Arabic.

"You should speak to them in Urdu only. And don't answer them if they reply in English—that is the only way they will learn." Thaya Jaan acts like Mustafa and I aren't in the room hearing his unwelcome advice.

My face grows warmer. If our uncle plans to ignore us unless we speak to him in Urdu, there's going to be a whole lot of silence around here.

85

"Well, we have been focusing more on their Arabic study than Urdu," Mama says. "You should hear them recite the Quran."

No, you really shouldn't!

"Mashallah, that's good." Thaya Jaan appears somewhat pacified.

"And, Bhai Jaan," Baba adds. "The kids are going to be in a recitation competition at the Islamic Center. We hoped you would help them prepare."

"Yes, yes, of course. I will help them."

My heart sinks as my chances of getting out of the competition shrink more than before. But I don't get to think about it for long as the sound of the adhan plays from the mosque-shaped clock in the den, filling the air with the call for the day's last prayer.

We all get up to prepare. I grab my favorite scarf while Mustafa spreads out colorful prayer rugs over the carpet. Thaya Jaan stands in the front to lead us all, taking Baba's usual spot, since he's both the eldest and most knowledgeable of the Quran.

I'm completely floored once Thaya Jaan starts to recite the familiar verses and finally understand where I got my musical talent. I've always known that it's definitely not from my parents. Baba's horribly tone-deaf, and Mama can barely carry a tune. But my uncle has a beautiful voice. As he speaks, he masterfully elongates certain words and varies the pitch of the Arabic phrases, which run together almost like a song. The sound rings through the room, reverberating off the walls, and echoes inside me.

Imam Malik recites really well and I always like listening to him, but hearing Thaya Jaan connects me to these verses in a way I've never experienced before. As I listen intently, I wish I could recite Arabic just like him. I imagine producing those melodious notes and pronouncing each letter properly—even with others listening—and the idea makes me happy. I end my prayers with a special wish.

Please, Allah, help the poor people in Pakistan who don't have enough to eat and protect my cousins in Pakistan. And please help me finally be able to pronounce the big haa.

11

"What's that?" Emily leans over to sniff in the direction of Soojin's lunch container. "It smells really good."

I almost drop my sandwich and stare in disbelief at Emily, who is sitting across from me, next to Soojin. *Now Emily likes Korean food all of a sudden?*

"It's my mom's famous bulgogi," Soojin replies. "Barbeque beef." Even though I know it's impossible, she's acting like she's forgotten all about what we always refer to as "the Incident." That was the day Soojin brought kimchee in her lunch in third grade and Emily and Julie pinched their noses and created a huge scene about how terrible it smelled.

"Can I try some?" Emily asks. She waves her fork near

Soojin's food a little too eagerly. Ever since she's become part of our wagon trail group, she's been sitting with us at lunch. I haven't said anything else about it to Soojin. She already knows what I think about her sudden friendliness toward Emily—I've dropped plenty of not-too-subtle hints about it. And either way, she's been acting like my opinion doesn't matter a whole lot.

"Sure." Soojin pushes the container toward Emily.

"*Mmmmm.* This is *sooo* good. Amina, you should try this," Emily gushes between chews.

"I've tried it. I have it all the time when I go to Soojin's house." I don't add that it's one of the only Korean dishes I really like. I don't touch anything sour or pickled, cabbage, fried eggs, or the spicy red sauce.

Emily pokes her fork into a baked chicken nugget that sits next to wilted green beans and an apple on her lunch tray.

"I wish my parents could cook like that."

"Doesn't your mom make those peanut butter cookies that you used to always bring in for class parties?" I can't help asking. Those cookies are amazing, and I used to always look forward to them in elementary school until they banned any party snacks with peanuts. "I thought she must be a great cook."

"No, I wish," Emily repeats. "Those cookies are like one of the only things she knows how to make, so she bakes them all the time. I'm pretty sick of them."

"What do you guys eat, then? Does your dad cook?" Soojin asks.

"We have a lot of frozen stuff. My dad grills sometimes. My grandma used to live with us and she made really good Polish food, but . . ." Emily pauses and fumbles with her napkin. ". . . she died a few years ago. My mom and grandma didn't get along, so my mom never wanted to learn how to cook like her. Now we never get to eat those kinds of things anymore."

"That's really sad," Soojin says. "My granddad lives with us."

"Yeah, that's really sad," I echo. Emily's life always seemed perfect to me, but now I wonder if maybe it isn't.

"After my grandma died, my mom went back to work

full-time. She works so much now that she doesn't have time for *anything* else. . . ." Emily's shoulders droop slightly.

Soojin's eyebrows furrow. "What does she do?"

"She's a lawyer. And she says that she's so lucky to have her career back that she has to work extra hard."

"That's rough," Soojin sympathizes. "My mom's a nurse, and we have the restaurant, so she's really busy too. But I'm lucky both my parents are really good cooks."

I picture Mr. Park in the kitchen, chopping up huge amounts of vegetables. He always hands me a piece of red pepper or broccoli and asks me to test it for freshness. And then Mrs. Park says something about how he should feed me butter instead to fatten me up.

"You can come over for dinner sometime if you want, Emily," Soojin adds.

"Really?" Emily brightens instantly, her green eyes sparkling.

"Yeah, sure." Soojin is nonchalant. "My parents love to cook for people."

"Thanks, Soojin."

I feel the spark of jealousy again as Emily and Soojin compare stories about living with grandparents and annoying little sisters. I nibble on a carrot stick as Emily talks about how her dad owns his own construction business and Soojin shares her parents' challenges running their deli.

It's happening. They're really becoming friends. I grip the side of the bench I'm sitting on so hard that my knuckles turn white. When did Soojin decide that Emily was better than "not so bad"? And when was she planning to tell *me*?

After eating, we're free to go outside to the courtyard for the last fifteen minutes of the lunch period. We walk together toward the big maple tree, which is Soojin's and my regular spot. Emily pauses in the shade of the tree.

"Okay, so I guess we'll see you later," I finally speak up. I want to be alone with Soojin, to see if it can be normal—like it always is when it's just the two of us. Things are all mixed up inside me, and I need some time to digest more than my lunch.

"Is it okay if I hang out with you guys?" Emily arches her eyebrows.

Soojin quickly glances at me, but either misreads my face or ignores it.

"Sure," she says.

"Great!" Emily finds a spot to sit down on, pushes away leaves, and settles onto the grass comfortably.

"There's something I wanted to ask you about . . . ," she starts to say.

"Yeah?" Soojin asks.

"It's a little embarrassing." Emily yanks on some crabgrass and blushes.

"Then you don't have to ask us," I mutter.

"Maybe I'll just talk to you later," Emily says. She directs her words at Soojin and tilts her head toward me slightly.

"No, no, whatever you can say to me, you can say to Amina. She's totally cool, and you can trust her." Soojin looks at me with wide eyes. "Right, Amina?"

"Yeah," I mumble.

"Okay," Emily says, looking unsure.

Soojin waits. "Go on," she prods.

"I . . . um . . . kind of like someone . . . ," Emily murmurs.

She focuses on Soojin as she speaks. I work hard to suppress a groan.

"And?" Soojin prompts.

"And I was wondering if you think he might like me." Emily's face turns pink as she speaks, and she giggles nervously. I glance at Soojin to see if she's as grossed out as me. But no, she seems fascinated!

Not only is Emily taking up important break time, but she's talking about *boys*? Soojin and I never waste time talking about stuff like that. Boys are the last thing I need to worry about, especially since most of them are so annoying.

"Who is it?" Soojin asks. She leans in to hear Emily better. I'm a little curious to know who has Emily acting so silly, but I try to act like I'm not.

"Well, he's in our social studies class . . ." Emily is clearly enjoying the spotlight. "And he's got blond hair . . ."

"Bradley?" I burst out. "Oh my God, you like *Bradley*?"

"*Eww!* No way." Emily scrunches up one side of her face in disgust.

"Seriously, Amina? You're really guessing Bradley?" Soojin scoffs.

"No! He was just the first blond boy I could think of. We've been spending way too much time with him lately."

"It's . . . Justin," Emily says in a whisper. And then she buries her face in her arm, like the Bollywood actresses always do when they are overreacting to a marriage proposal.

"I can see that," Soojin says. "He's kind of cute."

There's that word again. Puppies are cute. Babies are cute. But sixth-grade boys? *Yuck.* I've known Justin since the first grade and will never forget the first time he spoke to me. We were sitting together along the wall, with our legs sticking out in front of us. My white sandals were decorated with flowers and had little lights in them that glowed whenever I walked or banged my feet together.

"Look at that," Justin said, pointing toward my sandals.

I thought he was appreciating the special light-up quality of my shoes, until he added, "You have grass growing on your legs."

I was stunned.

"No I don't," I retorted in a small voice.

"Yeah, you do. Look!" Justin pointed to the fine dark hairs on my shins.

My eyes welled up, and I didn't know what to say. So I sat in silence against the wall, swallowed up in my shame, waiting to go home. Since that day, I've always felt a bit gorilla-like around Justin and make it a habit to avoid him. Thankfully he has never mentioned my hair or really talked to me again, but I have never forgotten it.

Five years later, Justin has a forest of his own growing on his legs and some fuzz on his upper lip. I picture his tousled dirty-blond hair, dark blue eyes, and very long neck. Justin is the kind of boy who is always in a jersey and gets picked first for every team during gym class. I don't understand what is cute about him at all.

"So . . . do you think he likes me, too?" Emily asks Soojin.

"Maybe," Soojin answers. "Have you ever even talked to him?" I don't wonder if Soojin is pretending to be interested anymore. She is totally into the conversation. I lean in closer to look at her.

Is she wearing lip gloss?

"We ride the same bus, and yesterday he asked me if I dropped my book. I didn't even have that book, so maybe he was trying to talk to me."

"Or maybe he really didn't know if you dropped the book," I point out. I want to talk about something else, anything else. Soojin and I haven't even had the chance to talk about the big-haired girl with the southern accent getting voted off *The Voice*. It was a huge shock, but I don't feel like talking about it in front of Emily.

"Then what happened?" Soojin leans in closer to Emily as if she hadn't heard what I said. The two of them continue to chatter about what Justin said or didn't say to Emily, when he looked or didn't look at her, and what all of that could mean. I shred dried leaves and listen, watching the pile of brown bits grow in front of me, feeling invisible. The wind slowly picks up the leaf bits and carries them away. And I wonder, if I slowly drifted off like them, would Soojin even notice?

12

"And . . . drumroll please . . ." Imam Malik pops into my Sunday school classroom.

"What is it?" Sami shouts, as he beats his fingers on his desk.

"We're adding a carnival on the day of the Quran competition!" Imam Malik smiles broadly while everyone cheers.

"There will be rides and games like last year, but we'll also have a dunk tank this time. It'll be a big fund-raiser for the Islamic Center, so be sure to tell your parents and register for the Quran competition if you haven't already."

"Who's going to be in the dunk tank?" Sami asks. Sami's the loudest kid in class.

"It's called Dunk-the-Imam, so yours truly will be inside."

"Will there be a bounce house?"

"And cotton candy?"

"Can I be in the dunk tank?"

Imam Malik looks helpless as our class bombards him with questions.

"That's enough, children," Sister Naima orders. "I'm sure you will get all the details later. Thank you, Imam Malik, for stopping by."

"Yes, of course. There will be a flyer with all the information, and the details will be on our website. Get back to work, and remember to practice hard for the competition!" Imam Malik dashes away. But Sister Naima has already lost control of the room. No one wants to do anything but talk about the carnival.

"Remember those awesome moon bounces with the big slides from last year? I hope they get those again," Mamadou says.

"Yeah! And that giant game of tug-of-war with adults versus kids? That was so fun," Sophia adds.

I can still feel the burn in my arms from pulling on the tug-of-war rope at the last carnival. The pain was worth it, though, because all the kids won and toppled the grown-ups. It was hilarious to watch the aunties and uncles, lying on the ground, laughing until they cried and blaming each other for letting go of the rope.

If I want to go to the carnival, there's no way I'm getting out of the Quran competition. The thought of it still makes my stomach turn, even though I've been sitting with Thaya Jaan every night after dinner, practicing my pronunciation and memorizing passages of the Quran. I don't feel like I'm getting any better. And it doesn't help that Thaya Jaan only speaks to me in Urdu during our lessons. Since I know he didn't want to hear me speak in English, I don't bother to ask the questions I want to, like how to pronounce the sounds like him and when to elongate certain words. I just don't have the Urdu vocabulary. Instead, I finish with him as quickly as possible and then go to my room and sing my heart out. After struggling with the Arabic, it helps me calm down to sing, even if it's kind of strange to go from Quran to Motown. I even made a video of myself singing a cover one time. But I deleted it before anyone, especially Rabiya, got ahold of it.

"Okay, okay! Enough about the carnival." Sister Naima hushes the room. "Whose turn is it to recite? Let's start with you, Sophia."

Luckily, by the time half the class has gotten through their turns, it's time for break, and I haven't been called on yet. When we're dismissed, I hurry out to find my friends. My stomach growls in anticipation of the jumbo samosas I saw someone carry into the school earlier. But as I walk through the bright hallway with colorful posters that read "Arabic Alphabet" and "The 99 Attributes of Allah," I spot Imam Malik and Mustafa standing in an empty alcove near the bookshelves. Imam Malik's back is to me, but he is waving his arms around. Mustafa is facing me, wearing jogging pants and high-top sneakers, with a sweatshirt. His face is red and stricken. Forgetting the samosa, I stand in the shadow of the bookshelves and listen unnoticed.

"I can't believe you, Mustafa! What were you thinking?

I'm so disappointed in you," Imam Malik is saying, his voice distressed.

"But I didn't do it . . . I swear," Mustafa sputters.

"You were there, weren't you?"

A long, tense pause follows as Mustafa's face tightens. "Yes," he mumbles. "I was there."

"And there was smoking going on, right?"

I gulp. *Smoking? Mustafa? How could he!*

"No! I mean, yes. I mean, I just wanted to play basketball. I wasn't smoking!"

"I saw the cigarettes with my own eyes, Mustafa." Imam Malik is firm.

"I know—*they* were smoking, but I wasn't. My class is so boring, and I just wanted to shoot the ball around. That's it, I promise."

"Even still, cutting class is a serious offense, Mustafa, boring or not. You shouldn't have been with those kids in the first place."

"I know," Mustafa hangs his head.

"Your parents trust you to make good decisions. This is hardly the place they expect you to fool around or get in trouble. Just think about how disappointed they are going to be."

"Imam Malik, please, please don't tell them." Mustafa's eyes are pleading. "My dad will flip out. I'll be in so much trouble, and . . . he'll make me quit the team at school." His words rush out in a stream.

Imam Malik shakes his head.

"I have to tell them, Mustafa. It's my responsibility."

Mustafa closes his eyes and rests his head against the wall for a second. Then he opens them again and speaks.

"I'm so sorry, Imam Malik. Really, I am. I should have known better. I shouldn't have done what I did. It was really stupid." Mustafa's voice is sincere, without a shred of the defensiveness that creeps in when he apologizes to our parents.

"Yes, it was. I expect more from you, Mustafa."

"I didn't mean to disappoint you, and I don't want

to hurt my parents. Is there any way you won't tell them? Please? I'll make it up to you."

"I don't know, Mustafa. You know I respect your father like a brother. . . ." Imam Malik clears his throat.

"If I do anything else wrong again . . . anything at all, then you can tell them everything. Please. My uncle is here from Pakistan and . . . ," Mustafa pleads. I imagine how upset Baba would be if his brother learned of this. And he and Mama have always made it clear that smoking is completely off limits. They would completely freak out.

"Okay." Imam Malik exhales slowly. "Just this once. I won't say anything, but I trust you not to do anything like this again. I'm serious. I'm going to talk to the other boys, and I don't want to see you around them anymore."

"Thank you! And I'm really sorry!" Mustafa starts to smile with relief, and then quickly regains his seriousness.

"Not so fast. I expect you to help out with this carnival, and to participate in this Quran competition, okay?"

"Yes, Imam Malik. Of course I will." Mustafa nods earnestly.

"And Mustafa—are you okay? Is everything all right at home? Is there anything you want to tell me?"

"Yeah, I'm fine." Mustafa shifts on his feet. "Everything is good."

"You know that if you ever need to talk about anything, I'm here. This place is your home, Mustafa, and everyone here is like your family."

"I know," Mustafa looks ashamed and grateful at once.

Imam Malik turns and puts his hand on Mustafa's back to lead him outside when he notices me.

"Oh! Have you been standing there for long?" He looks alarmed, and then tries to relax his face. "Mustafa and I were just having a chat. Why don't you two run outside and get a snack. Break is almost over."

And then he rushes away, muttering something about checking on the announcements. I stand in place and stare at my brother. Then without warning, I burst into tears.

"What are you doing?" Mustafa barks. He glances around to make sure no one is watching us. "Why the heck are you crying?"

The tears roll down my face, and my breath comes out in spurts.

"I . . . you . . . smoking kills!" I sob. I know I look like a big baby for crying but can't help it as I think of him leaning against a building, a cigarette dangling from his lips. What will be next? Drugs?

"What? Didn't you hear me tell Imam Malik I wasn't smoking?" Mustafa sounds like he doesn't know whether to laugh or yell at me.

"Is it true?" I manage to stop crying, but now my nose is running, and I wipe it with the end of my sleeve.

"Yes, Amina."

"Well, do you *want* to smoke?" I sniff.

"No, Amina. It's disgusting. Come on, let's go." He pulls on my arm, leading me to the door.

"Listen." He stops suddenly. "You're not going to tell on me, are you?"

"No." The last thing I want is to say anything about this to our parents.

"Promise?" Mustafa stares into my eyes.

"If you promise you won't smoke."

"Deal." Mustafa puts his arm around my shoulders. "Come on, crybaby, let's go get some food before they run out."

I've lost my appetite, but I wipe my eyes and nose again, try to hide that I've been crying, and walk outside with him.

13

After dinner, as I sit on my piano bench and start to practice, my mind wanders back to the ride home from the Islamic Center. Baba was filling Thaya Jaan in on plans for the carnival and how he was inviting local churches, synagogues, temples, and interfaith organizations to attend. I wondered if Soojin's Korean church would participate again this year and made a mental note to ask her about it. But then I thought about her and Emily, and whether Soojin was starting to think the two of them had more in common than we did. *Emily goes to church too.*

Mustafa sat in the backseat beside me, lost in thought, and stared out the window. At dinner, when Mama asked how Sunday school was, he said "fine" in his usual mono-syllabic way but gave me a warning look that I knew meant I should keep my mouth shut.

Now, sitting alone, I'm drained from the day's events. I glance over at Mustafa sitting on the sofa, finishing up his chemistry homework. Hunched over his books in his sweatshirt and cap, he looks younger, like the old Mustafa I've always known.

I open up the piano cabinet and start to play a compila-tion of pop songs from the 1960s that Ms. Holly gave me to practice on Friday during music class.

"I know you don't want to sing in the concert, but it would be wonderful if you could play piano and accompany the singers," she asked with a hopeful expression.

I wanted to say, "But I do want to sing. More than any-thing." But I didn't. Instead, I agreed to do it, took the sheet music, and shoved it into my bag. As much as I love playing piano, it stinks to be stuck in the background while other people shine onstage, a soundtrack no one pays attention to, like the music piped into *The Voice*. My only consolation is that at least I don't get nervous playing the piano in front of an audience. I've done plenty of piano recitals over the years, where Mrs. Kuckleman showcases all her students one by one, from the little ones who slowly pick out "Happy Birthday" to the most advanced players who master Mozart. And since I'm sitting on the bench and focusing on the notes on a page and not the faces in the crowd, I can forget that there are even people there.

"Is that Elvis?" Baba asks as I press the keys.

"Yeah. We're doing music from the sixties through the eighties for our concert."

"*Uh huh uh* . . . I'm all shook up . . . ," Baba sings in a fake deep voice as he passes through the family room, making me laugh for the first time since that afternoon. The combination of playing and his goofy singing makes me feel better.

But later that night, as I brush my teeth in the bathroom, I overhear Baba and Thaya Jaan talking in the guest room next door.

"All this music all the time. You shouldn't let Amina do so much singing and piano," Thaya Jaan says.

I stop brushing and strain to hear every word, trying to follow.

"But, Bhai Jaan, she is so talented. Her music teachers say she is really quite gifted."

"Yes, but music is forbidden in Islam. It's a waste of time and has no benefit. Instead of filling her head with music, she should focus on memorizing Quran."

The toothpaste suddenly tastes bitter. I spit it out and wait to hear what Baba will say. Surely he'll say the things he's always told me, like how music makes him feel closer to God and that my talent is a gift from Allah.

But all Baba says is, "Yes, Bhai Jaan," and then he stays quiet. I am numb.

Is Thaya Jaan right? Am I doing something wrong?

As leftover tears from earlier in the day mix with the water I splash on my face, I regret hearing a word of their conversation. I crawl into bed, pull my quilt over my head, and try to slow the pounding of my heart.

14

"Amina! Where are you? Come down here!" Mama calls from the kitchen.

I slide off my bed and go down the stairs. Mama is wiping the counters down with a rag, even though they are already gleaming.

"What have you been doing since you came home? Why are you hiding up in your room?"

"Cleaning it."

"On a Friday afternoon?" Mama's eyes narrow. "Are you feeling okay?"

"Yeah." I stare at my socks.

"Are you sure? What's the matter?"

"Nothing. I'm fine." I see Mama's concerned expression and try to smile. I don't know how to explain how I'm feeling. It's not exactly sick, but not exactly normal, either. I just feel . . . tired.

"Okay, well we're taking Thaya Jaan out to dinner tonight. Go run up and get ready. Put on that nice yellow shirt."

"Where are we going?"

"There's a new Thai restaurant that Baba wants to try."

Yum! Thai food is one of my favorites. I love getting noodles with peanut sauce and shrimp and spicy chicken skewers.

"What about Mustafa? He isn't home yet." I've hardly seen him all week, since he's been at practice every afternoon until pretty late. Plus I've been steering clear of the family room after dinner. I don't want to run into Thaya Jaan.

"He is going out for pizza with his team after his game tonight. They had to play in Oak Creek."

"Oh." I'm suddenly less interested in dinner. I picture myself eating my noodles in silence as my parents talk to

Thaya Jaan in Urdu about the proper ways to raise children or about Pakistani politics.

I go upstairs and dig the yellow shirt out of my dresser, switching on my iPod out of habit. As the music fills the room, my spirits start to lift . . . until Thaya Jaan's words come back to me. *Music is forbidden.* I quickly turn it off again and sit on my bed, staring at the music books and sheets lying scattered on the floor. I can't shake the uneasy feeling that has settled on me like dust for days—have I been doing something wrong, or un-Islamic, by spending so much of my time singing and playing piano?

"Let's go, Amina!" Baba calls, jingling his car keys. He always does that when he's in a hurry to leave.

When I get to the garage, Thaya Jaan is standing next to Baba, wearing a white shalwar kameez with a black-band collar vest on top. He has a black furry hat propped atop his head that looks like a giant paper boat. I figure he dressed up to go to the mosque for Friday prayers and is still in the same clothes. And as mean-spirited as I feel, I wish he weren't here.

"There you are, geeta," Baba says. "Where have you been hiding?"

"Don't you think galaree is a more suitable name for your daughter today?" Thaya Jaan says with the hint of a smile. Baba chuckles in agreement.

My cheeks burn, and I brush past my uncle and climb into the backseat of the car without saying a word. *Is Thaya Jaan making fun of me?*

Mama gets into the backseat with me, giving Thaya Jaan the front, out of respect. That suits me perfectly, since I don't want to be sitting next to him anyway. As we start backing out of the garage, I lean over and whisper to my mother.

"What does galaree mean?"

Mama touches my bright yellow blouse and smiles.

"It means canary. You look like a little songbird."

"Oh." I don't get the joke or want Thaya Jaan to comment on my shirt, my singing, or anything else about me. The weight of his words presses down on me all over again, and I try to act interested, as Mama is super chatty and jokes around with me on our ride, but my heart isn't in it.

15

Early the next morning I find Mustafa in the kitchen. He's chewing on oatmeal with peanut butter mixed into it. I catch a whiff of his sporty, fresh-scented shower gel and notice his hair is wet. He's sitting in a T-shirt and shorts, even though it's chilly in the house and I'm wearing fleece pajamas.

"What are you doing up so early?" I ask. Mustafa usually sleeps in until noon on Saturdays.

"I went for a run. I need to do some extra conditioning."

"Why? You already made the team, didn't you?"

"Yeah, but if I want to be a starter I have to show the coach that I'm working hard and improving."

"Aren't you the only freshman on the team?"

"Yup." Mustafa's spoon scrapes the bottom of his bowl.

"Doesn't that make you feel good?"

"That's not the point, Amina. I think I can be the best player on the team. I just need to work harder than everyone else."

I wonder if Mustafa gets nervous before his games, knowing that everyone is watching him and that at any moment he could fall on his face or shoot an air ball. If he does, he does a good job hiding it. I kind of want to tell him that I'm proud of him for making the team. And that I wish he had been at dinner last night. But I don't. We don't say stuff like that to each other.

Baba walks into the kitchen, wearing his bathrobe. "So you're awake. We need to talk." He sits down at the table across from Mustafa like he means business.

"Since you cannot remember when to come home at night, your mother and I have decided that you're not going out with the team anymore. You go to the games but then come home." Baba speaks firmly. When we got home from dinner, I went upstairs and got into bed. I didn't hear when

Mustafa got back, but it must have been pretty late.

"But, Baba, they're my friends . . ." Mustafa starts to protest.

"We'd prefer you spend more time with people your own age who are a better influence. And with Yusuf and with other boys from the Islamic Center."

If Baba only knew about the boys from the Islamic Center.

"I'm not a little kid anymore. You don't need to plan playdates for me." Mustafa scowls.

"Watch it," Baba warns. "You're lucky. I was so angry I was going to make you quit the team, but your Thaya Jaan convinced me to let you play."

"Thaya Jaan? Really?" Mustafa says.

"Yes. He said that you had to take responsibility for your actions, but that you also have a commitment to your team."

Wait. So Thaya Jaan is anti music but he is pro basketball?

"If you can show us that you can follow the rules, then we can talk about this again when we feel it is time. But until then, this is final."

"Okay, Baba," Mustafa says quietly. I'm glad to see that

he isn't starting a fight. We all know that would be a losing battle.

"And I need you to understand that we make rules for a reason, not to punish you."

"I know, I know. I get it. Can I go now?" I wince as Mustafa's tone grows rude. But Baba just nods. Mustafa picks up his empty bowl and drops it in the sink. I watch my father slump in his chair in his striped bathrobe, with his bed head and black-and-white stubble on his chin. He seems worn out, even though the day has just started. I get up from my seat and put my arms around him as Mustafa goes up to his room.

Mama walks into the kitchen, wearing a freshly ironed shalwar kameez. Since Thaya Jaan has been staying with us, she doesn't hang around in her pajamas and robe on weekend mornings like usual. And she certainly doesn't smile as much. I don't blame her.

"You guys already ate? I was going to make eggs."

"I'll have some." Baba absently strokes my hair.

I think about Baba letting Thaya Jaan tell him to let

Mustafa play on the team. Did Baba agree with him, or was it that he couldn't say no? I decide I need to know some answers for myself and, after taking a deep breath, ask the question that has been sitting on my chest like a lead blanket for the past week.

"Baba, why does God hate music?"

"What?" Mama says. She puts down her spatula and turns to face me. "Where did you get that idea?"

"I heard Thaya Jaan telling Baba last week that it was haram for me to play music."

"Saleem! Are you hearing this? What did he say? And what did you say to him?" Mama hisses softly, even though the shower is running in the bathroom upstairs and Thaya Jaan won't be able to hear us.

"Well, he was just saying that music is forbidden. I know we don't agree with that interpretation of Islam, but I couldn't say anything to him," Baba mumbles.

Mama lets out an exasperated sigh and comes over to the table. She kneels to be eye level with me and holds me by the shoulders. "Is that why I haven't heard you practicing your piano or singing this week? You are *not* doing anything wrong. God does not hate music. I don't believe that, or that it's wrong for you to play or to sing. Why would he give you so much talent then?"

I really want to believe her, but I look at Baba and wait to see what he has to say.

"I'm sorry, geeta. I guess I should have said what I thought right then. The truth is I agree with your mother, and I do believe my brother is wrong about this, okay?"

"Okay. But then why did he say that?"

"Your Thaya Jaan has some religious views that are strict. Like the not-participating-in-Halloween thing. Some Muslims are extra careful and avoid anything that they think might be wrong in any way. Music at the time of the Prophet's life was thought to be a harmful influence."

I kind of understand, but it's still strange to have witnessed Baba pretending to agree with his brother. It must have been part of the wanting-everyone-to-be-perfect-and-never-disagreeing stuff.

"There is some music out there that I do think is

inappropriate—like music with bad language—but that's different," he continued. "Your music is wonderful."

I nod.

"You have to talk to him," Mama says with a frown. "I respect Bhai Jaan for his beliefs, but this is too much. We have a right to teach our children our values. What if Amina had never said anything to us and thought she was doing something wrong for loving music?"

I wait to see how Baba will react. He listens quietly and then looks lost in thought.

"You're right," he finally says. "I will talk to him."

16

"What's up with Emily and Soojin? Are they like best friends or something now?" Bradley points to where the two of them are sitting together at the mapping station Mrs. Barton had set up, examining the Oregon Trail. His words spark a fresh shock of jealousy that courses through my veins like I had stuck my pen into an electrical socket.

"No, they're just working together," I reply, knowing full well that isn't true either. Soojin and Emily are definitely friends now; there's no denying that. But Soojin is still *my* best friend, and everyone knows it. *I hope Emily knows it too.*

"I can go ask Soojin to switch places with me. You can

be with your BFF, and I can be near Emily." Bradley's blue eyes are teasing.

"Really? You want to be near Emily?"

"Yeah. You're pretty cool, but I wouldn't mind getting closer to Emily, if you know what I mean." He jabs me in the side with his elbow.

"*Ow!* I don't know what you mean," I start to say. "Wait a minute—are you saying that you . . . *like* Emily?

"No way. All I'm saying is that Emily is . . . you know, kind of . . . pretty."

I look over at Emily. Her neatly trimmed blond hair is held in place with a brown leather headband. Her eyes are nice, bright green, set in an angular face with high cheekbones and just the right number of freckles. If I were forced to admit it, she is actually kind of pretty. But I've never noticed that before.

"Forget it, Bradley. Emily likes Justin," I blurt out, then clamp my mouth shut.

Uh-oh.

"What? Emily said she likes Justin?" Bradley leans in

closer with wide eyes, giving me his full attention.

"What? No. I mean, I don't know." My cheeks burn.

"Wow. Well, I guess it makes sense. He is a jock and everything. I just thought Emily might like someone . . . smarter." Bradley sulks.

"Listen, I don't know who she likes or doesn't. It was just a guess . . . isn't Justin really popular? A lot of girls like him," I say with growing desperation.

Bradley eyes me like he doesn't believe a word of it.

"Don't say anything to anyone, okay?" I beg, dread spreading through my insides. What if Emily's secret gets out? That would be awful. Soojin told her that I could be trusted.

I am *trustworthy. Usually.*

"Yeah, yeah, okay. Who cares anyway? Let's get this wagon moving! We're not in last place anymore!" Bradley pulls out the sheet with our assignment for the day and starts reading the instructions aloud, his eyes intense with concentration.

I let myself breathe again. Bradley has moved on, and, knowing him, the conversation will quickly be forgotten. He isn't going to tell anyone anything. It isn't his style.

17

"Isn't it taking forever for Mrs. Barton to get our work back to us? We took that unit test more than two weeks ago," Emily complains during lunch. She's sitting across from me, rummaging through her reusable green lunch bag.

"My dad noticed that our grades are getting posted online much later than usual," Soojin agrees. "But forget about that. Guess what tomorrow is?"

"What?" Emily and I ask in unison.

"Our swearing-in ceremony! Remember I told you guys it was October twentieth? I can't believe it's already here. I'm going to miss school. And this is the last day you'll be seeing me as Soojin."

"That's so exciting . . . Susan!" Emily gushes with a little giggle as she utters Soojin's future name. "Isn't it, Amina?"

"Yeah, that's really great." I'm completely fake as I try to match Emily's enthusiasm. But I just can't call Soojin Susan yet. I hate that idea too much.

"My mom is so psyched about the party she's throwing to celebrate." Soojin describes the heaps of red, white, and blue decorations her mother has been collecting since Independence Day.

"My aunt always brings this cake for our Fourth of July barbeque where she puts strawberries and blueberries on whipped cream to make an American flag," Emily says. "You should totally make that!"

"Good idea. And you guys are both invited."

"Let's celebrate right now." Emily pulls out a bag of her mother's peanut butter cookies. "Have some, Amina," she offers, pushing them toward me. "I know you like these."

"Thanks," I say. I take one, touched that she remembered.

"Hey, Em-i-ly!" A loud voice calls out from the other

end of the lunchroom. It's Luke, wearing an ugly sneer.

"What?" Emily turns her head toward him nervously.

"Want to come over here and sit next to your . . . lover boy?" Luke laughs and throws a potato chip at Justin, who's sitting across from him. Justin surveys the room, catches a glimpse of Emily, and then looks away. His ears turn cherry red.

"You're so weird." Emily coolly flips her head around and turns her attention to her bagel as if nothing out of the ordinary has happened.

What did that little twerp do? I scan the crowd for Bradley, who is slouched in his seat at the table to my left. His eyes widen as they meet mine, and he ducks his head. Sheepishly, he mouths the word "oops" to me. My heart thrashes wildly in my chest. *How quickly will Emily trace the leak back to me?*

"Your boo is right here waiting for you, Emily!" Luke jeers as the boys around him laugh like hyenas. Kyle purses his freckled face and makes loud kissing noises.

"No, I'm not!" Justin yelps as Kyle tousles his hair. "I am not!" he repeats, his voice now rough with anger. He stands up, brushing everyone off him, and moves to the other end of the table, where he sits and fumes.

Emily acts like she hasn't heard a thing, but I can see her flinch ever so slightly at Justin's words, and her face turns a shade pinker. Hearing all of the commotion, Mrs. Greenwich, the lunchroom attendant, comes over to hush the tables.

"What's going on here? If you don't settle down, I'm going to separate you," she threatens.

"How did Luke find out?" Soojin whispers to Emily as everyone quickly quiets. "Who else did you tell about Justin?"

Emily just shakes her head slightly, still staring at her sandwich. She blinks hard, trying not to cry.

The next few minutes drag on in a tense silence. I pretend to nibble on my cookie for as long as possible, but the peanut butter tastes like dirt. Afraid to look at Emily, I walk slowly over to the trash can to throw the rest of it away along with my napkin and milk carton. There, I take a few deep breaths and steel myself for whatever will happen next.

We're dismissed for the last ten minutes of lunch, and I

walk out to the courtyard with Soojin and Emily with feet as heavy as lead. Luke runs by us with a smirk, while Emily holds her head high and refuses to look in his direction. But as soon as we are on the other side of the building, hidden from view, she spins around to face me.

"How could you?" Emily demands. Her green eyes are ablaze with a mixture of hurt and fury. "I trusted you, and now look what happened!"

I gulp and start to pour out the heartfelt apology I know I owe her.

"Listen, I just . . ."

"Hold on!" Soojin holds up her hand. "You can't just go and accuse Amina like that! I already told you, you can trust her with anything."

I shut my mouth and stand there like an idiot, looking back and forth at Emily, seething with anger, and Soojin, whose unshakable faith in me makes me feel like the most horrible person in the world.

"But I didn't tell anyone else but you guys, and you didn't say anything, did you?" Emily asks Soojin.

"No, of course not." Soojin sounds indignant.

Emily starts to cry, and large salty tears flow down her cheeks. "I'm so embarrassed I could die!" she howls. "I'm sorry, Amina, but I don't know how they found out, and I just assumed it was you."

"What about Julie?" Soojin asks. "Do you think she said anything to anyone?"

"I never told Julie! I don't even really talk to her anymore," Emily wails. "I can't trust her like I do you guys."

A massive wave of guilt almost knocks me over as I realize Emily really does consider us friends—both Soojin *and* me. My mind starts to race. Even though Emily followed Julie around and acted like her chamchee for all those years, it doesn't count for anything anymore. They aren't even close, and it looks like they barely hang out. Maybe Emily just got smarter and realized she wants new friends in middle school. Real friends, like Soojin and me. *But wait—am I even a real friend?* Not only did I tell Emily's secret and watch her be humiliated in front of the entire grade without doing anything to help, now I was actually letting her apologize to me.

"Then how do you think Luke found out?" Soojin presses.

"I don't know. Maybe someone heard us talking about it."

"What do you think, Amina? I don't remember anyone being around when we were talking. Do you?" Soojin peers directly into my eyes.

"Well, not exactly," I hear myself saying in a tiny voice. I pause, trying to swallow the sawdust in my throat, as something inside me pushes me to go on. "But . . . maybe . . . somehow . . . someone by accident . . . someone might have heard me talking to Bradley. . . ."

"Wait! What? Bradley? What were you talking to Bradley about?" Soojin asks.

"He was saying that he thought Emily was pretty or something," I start to explain.

"Eww!" Emily moans between sobs.

"I know, right? And so, I was trying to tell him that he didn't have a chance."

"And?" Soojin pushes me to go on.

"And . . . I kind of ended up saying that Emily liked

Justin. I didn't mean to. Honest. It just came out of my mouth." Even though it's true, I can't believe the words I'm saying.

"How could you do that?" Soojin explodes. She stretches out her arms in exasperation and then clamps them over her head. "I can't believe you, Amina! What the hell were you thinking?"

I'm as still as a statue. *Soojin has never yelled at me before.*

"Yeah, how could you!" Emily repeats. "I would *never* do that to you." Her face twists with anger.

"I know. I'm really, really sorry." I hang my head.

"Now what am I supposed to do?" Emily starts crying again.

"Nothing. You don't have to do anything." Soojin puts a protective arm around Emily. And then she turns her back on me.

"What do you mean?" Emily whimpers.

"You were totally cool at lunch, and no one knows if anything Luke said is true or not. Just ignore everyone like you did and act like it was all a big lie."

"I'll try. But now I know . . . Justin doesn't like me." Emily wilts even further.

"You don't know that." Soojin strokes Emily's back. "Maybe he was just embarrassed. Who would want to admit anything in front of those jerks?"

"Yeah, maybe now he'll even realize that he *does* like you," I add. I inch toward them with a hopeful expression.

"Or maybe he'll never talk to me again!" Emily retorts harshly. Soojin whips her head around and gives me a look that warns me to step back.

So I step back. Soojin is really angry, and she has a right to be. I watch as she continues to comfort Emily, feeling unwelcome, but unsure whether it would look worse if I just walked away. So I stand there awkwardly until the bell rings to signal the end of lunch and fidget with the straps on my bag. The whole time, Soojin doesn't turn around to look at me. But as the bell rings, with her encouragement, Emily dries her tears, takes deep breaths, and prepares to walk back into the school as if nothing happened.

Now I feel like crying, but I don't let myself.

"Soojin, listen," I try to say as my best friend just walks right by me. After a few steps Soojin stops and turns around.

"I don't want to talk to you right now." She sounds more sad than angry.

And then she continues walking, leaving me there. I eventually trail behind them toward the doors to the school and turn in the opposite direction to go my locker. My insides are churning, and I want to throw up. Instead of going to class, I decide to go to the nurse's office and lie down until it is time to go home. Even though I know it's cowardly, I can't bear to face Soojin or Emily again.

18

"Amina! Where are you?" Mama calls from the kitchen. "I need your help."

"In here," I reply from where I'm sitting at the dining room table and give my uncle a weak smile. "I'm practicing with Thaya Jaan."

"Okay. But when you're done I need you to set the plates out for me. And where in the world have your father and brother gone?"

Baba has a way of disappearing for hours whenever Mama throws a dinner party. He usually finds some kind of urgent business to take him to the electronics or hardware store, like a missing speaker wire or special kind of lightbulb that needs replacing. This Saturday morning, he's taken Mustafa with him, while Mama prepares for the dinner party they are holding in honor of Thaya Jaan's visit. She's already done a lot of cooking over the past few nights, and the kitchen counters are covered with piles of onions, garlic bulbs, and chili peppers, along with jars of spices and gleaming serving dishes.

"We are almost finished," Thaya Jaan volunteers. "Let's review this surah one more time."

I read through the page, paying extra attention to the flow and rhythm of the verses. The repetition of sounds in this particular passage, a surah called Humazah, makes it easy to memorize.

"Very good!" Thaya Jaan says. "You are improving."

"What does it mean?" The rhymes sound so pretty, I'm sure the meaning is too.

"This surah is a harsh warning from Allah to those who do backbiting of their brothers. God tells us that nothing, not even all of a person's wealth, will save them from his wrath."

"Backbiting?" I don't know this word. And even though Thaya Jaan is speaking in English for a change, it isn't helping much.

"When you speak ill of people behind their backs, or say things about them that you should not," Thaya Jaan explains.

A shiver runs down my spine.

"Shall we review it one last time?"

I shake my head, too upset to speak.

Is there a special punishment for me?

Thaya Jaan keeps going. "This surah is just a reminder for all of us to watch what we say and not to be arrogant."

"But what if you did it by accident? What if you didn't know what you were saying?" I'm ashamed to say the words.

"I don't understand. How do you say something by accident?"

Mama walks out of the kitchen and stops when she sees my face.

"What happened?" she asks Thaya Jaan.

"Nothing. I just told her the meaning of the surah."

"It's my fault, Mama. I did a really mean thing to Emily, and I'm a backbiter, and I'm going to be punished . . ." I trail off.

"Hold on now. Come with me." Mama drags me away by the hand and flashes Thaya Jaan a warning look as we go up the stairs. When we get to her room, Mama sits me on the bed next to her.

"Okay, tell me what happened. Did Thaya Jaan say something again?"

I pour out the entire story about Emily and Soojin, starting with the school project and ending with what happened in the lunchroom. Mama listens intently, interrupting a few times to ask questions or to slow me down.

"So did you tell Emily's secret on purpose, to get back at her for becoming Soojin's friend?" she asks finally.

I think about it for a moment. "No, I was just annoyed with Bradley."

"Did you want Bradley or the others to tease her?"

"No."

"Well then, why did you tell him?"

"It just popped out of my mouth, I promise. I just wasn't thinking. I know I don't like Emily . . . well, I didn't like Emily before, and I guess I was kind of jealous of her becoming friends with Soojin. But I would never try to hurt her on purpose. And I'm starting to think that maybe she's not that bad. I actually think she might be . . . pretty nice."

"I believe you." Mama brushes the hair out of my face and fixes the collar of my shirt like she did when I was a little girl. "You're not a mean person, Amina, and you never have been. You just made a mistake. Everyone does sometimes."

"Yeah, but what about what the surah says?"

"What surah?"

"Humazah."

Mama laughs. "Is that what got you so upset? It is a strong surah, but it's not describing you, silly girl. You weren't being evil or trying to spread rumors about Emily."

"No, I wasn't," I agree, feeling a little better. "But what do I do now? Everyone's so mad at me."

"Just ask for forgiveness—from God, and from your friends." Mama is solemn as she gives me the simple advice.

"I did. I said sorry right away. But they were both still really angry at me. Soojin was furious."

Mama shrugs. "Well, it makes sense that they're upset with you. Wouldn't you feel the same way if someone told one of your secrets? What happened when you saw them in school yesterday?"

"Emily ignored me. I tried to say hi, but she acted like she didn't hear me. So then I wrote her a long note and left it in her cubby. Soojin wasn't in school because her family was at their ceremony to become citizens."

"Oh, did that happen already? That's wonderful. I'll have to congratulate them the next time I see them."

"Yeah." I don't mention the part about Soojin changing her name. Mama wouldn't be crazy about that idea. But I feel awful that Soojin's family is having this big moment after waiting for so long, and I'm not even talking to my best friend. That is, if Soojin even considers me her best friend any more.

"Why don't you invite Soojin and her family to come to the carnival next week? Their church participated last year, right? That could be a nice gesture," Mama suggests. "Besides, Imam Malik and Baba want it to be an interfaith event again."

"I don't know. I guess I'll see her at school on Monday." It makes me nervous to think about facing Soojin, or Susan, for the first time after our fight. And since my mother reminded me of the carnival, it means the Quran competition is fast approaching. Even though I feel a little better about the way my lessons with Thaya Jaan are going, I certainly don't feel prepared enough to get up in front of hundreds of people to recite a surah. And now that I know what it means, there's no way I'm choosing surah Humazah. I wouldn't be able to get through it.

Mama looks at me with sympathy. "If Soojin is truly your best friend, she'll forgive you. You'll just have to wait and see. And you have to trust that just because she makes new friends doesn't mean she stops caring about you. Now come downstairs and give me a hand. Everyone will be here in a couple hours."

19

"Everything looks delicious." Salma Auntie carries the last steaming dish to the dining table, and then stands back to admire the elaborate feast. Her family was the first to arrive for the party, and she immediately got to work. She threw on one of Mama's aprons, rolled up her sleeves, and tied her hair back into a bun. That also meant that she felt like she could give me orders like my own mother.

"I hope it tastes good too," Mama says. "Amina, can you tell everyone to come and eat?"

Rabiya helped me stack napkins between the fancy china plates earlier, and we now pass them out as everyone comes into the dining room. Mustafa pours an assortment of sodas and water into plastic cups and sets them out on the counter.

Thaya Jaan walks into the kitchen, and I hand him a plate.

"No, not yet. Let the others take their food first. I can wait," he says, standing aside.

"No, Bhai Jaan, you are the guest of honor. Please take your food," Mama insists. I heard her come downstairs after our talk and explain to Thaya Jaan why I had freaked out. Even though she didn't actually apologize to him, I know Mama felt bad for assuming Thaya Jaan had said something to upset me.

When it's my turn, I fill my plate with rice, shami kabob, lentils, and butter chicken, skipping the cauliflower and salad, and pile the naan high before carefully carrying it downstairs to the basement. Rabiya, Yusuf, and the other kids are already camped in front of the TV with their food.

Mustafa joins a few minutes later, plopping down on our beat-up leather sofa next to Yusuf.

"There's nothing good on," Yusuf announces after flipping through all the channels.

"Isn't there a basketball game?" Mustafa asks.

"Nooo!" Rabiya whines.

"I want *SpongeBob*," a little boy named Jamal says, chewing on a piece of naan.

"How about we tell scary stories?" Yusuf suggests.

"No way," Rabiya refuses. "Last time I had nightmares for days."

I agree. Yusuf tells the scariest stories ever. The worst one was about severed hands of bodies that were dug up from graves. The hands came to life and would tickle people to death. I still think about that whenever we pass a graveyard.

"What are you going to be for Halloween this year, Amina?" Rabiya asks. "I'm going to be a peacock. My mom is making me a huge feathered tail."

I sigh as I remember my big plans for Halloween with Soojin. *Will she still want to go trick-or-treating with me, or someone else now?*

"I said, what are you going to be?" Rabiya repeats.

"I don't know."

"Really? Why not? I thought you and Soojin always came up with great costumes?"

"Yeah, well, we might be ketchup and mustard bottles this year," I mumble.

"If you don't, we can do something together . . . like the peacock and the . . . What would go well with a peacock?" Rabiya's face scrunches up in thought.

"How about a chicken?" Yusuf volunteers.

"Or a pirate?" Mustafa adds.

Everyone takes turns coming up with ridiculous costume partner ideas for me.

"A toothbrush!" Jamal offers.

I laugh and look around the room, feeling lighter for the first time since lunch last week. *Maybe I should just forget about Soojin and Emily.* I try to imagine myself in school without them, concentrating on my work, eating lunch with Allison or Margot. Maybe I'd manage to get through my school week, and then I could enjoy my free time with Rabiya, Dahlia, and my other weekend friends. That could work.

But then I think about how Soojin has been the best part of school ever since she moved to Greendale. I'd be miserable if we weren't good friends and don't know how I'd survive middle school without her. *I'll apologize again and see what happens. Mama said if Soojin is really my best friend, she'll forgive me.* I'm not sure it's that simple. But I hope she's right.

20

I stir, hearing hushed voices outside my bedroom door.

"It'll be okay. I'll be back soon," Baba is saying.

I flop onto my other side, pulling my comforter up over me. It's still dark outside and doesn't feel like morning.

"The police are there already. Malik is frantic—he wants Hamid and me to come right away. Don't worry; I'll call you when I know more."

Police? I'm wide awake now. The alarm clock next to my bed glows red with the time: 4:47 a.m.

"Be careful, please." Mama's voice is still thick with sleep.

"I will." Baba's footsteps descend the stairs, muffled by

the carpet. I hear the garage door open and his car engine roar to life.

"Mama?" I get up and tiptoe into my parents' room. Mama sits in her checkered fleece robe, tense on the edge of her bed.

"Why are you awake? Go back to sleep." Mama tries to sound like everything is okay, but I know it isn't.

"What happened?" I lean close against her like I used to when I was little.

Mama's face is gray. She looks at me, starts to say something, and then lets out a deep sigh instead.

"What?" I ask again, scared.

"Someone broke into the Islamic Center and did some damage. Imam Malik called and asked Baba to come right away."

My fists clench. "Did anyone get hurt?"

"No. Thank God no one was there when it happened."

"Will we still have Sunday school?" I don't know why that is my first thought, but I planned on giving Rabiya back the book she was reading for a book report. She left it on the floor of the basement during the party last night.

"No, no Sunday school today." Mama touches the bed next to her. "Why don't you lie down with me?"

I crawl into my dad's side of the bed, which smells faintly of his cologne, and drift into a light sleep. Mama rises shortly after for the dawn prayers, and I also hear Thaya Jaan running the water in the hall bathroom. Finally I fall into a deep sleep until the shrill ringing of the phone next to my head wakes me up again a few hours later.

"Hello?" I ask, after fumbling to pick up the receiver.

"Amina, this is Salma Auntie. Where is your mother?"

I hand Mama the phone and listen to their conversation.

"He said the main hall is badly damaged." Mama's voice, a low whisper, quavers. I picture the Islamic Center—the two-story community building holds the main hall, where lectures, weddings, and all the parties take place. The first floor also has a small kitchen, office, and library, but Mama says she doesn't know what shape they are in. I spend most of my time upstairs in the Sunday school classrooms, which Mama tells Auntie are covered with graffiti. I try to process what I'm hearing but can't believe it is true. *Why would anyone want to ruin our beautiful center? What would they get out of that?*

"The mosque is the worst part," Mama says, trembling.

I imagine the beautiful gold-domed mosque and minarets that stand beside the community building.

"The fire department got there in time before it burned down, but Saleem said it's really bad," Mama says. "I can't believe it, Salma. I just can't believe this happened. Every time I hear about things like this in other places, I think, it'll never happen in Greendale."

I shiver as I hear the anguish in my mother's tone, even as I lie buried under the down comforter on my parents' bed.

"Are you going, Salma?" asks Mama. "Yes, yes, you're right."

Mama hangs up the phone and reaches past me for the tissue box on the side table.

"Get dressed and wake up Mustafa," she says as she wipes her nose. "We're going over there."

21

Police cars line the driveway to the Islamic Center, making everything I've heard suddenly very real and even more terrifying. I'm certain that Mustafa, who's on the other side of me in the backseat of our minivan, can hear my heart beating through my thick jacket. Thaya Jaan has been clicking his prayer beads the whole ride.

"There's Saleem." Mama points toward the main entrance of the community hall. She parks the car in the nearly empty lot, and we all pile out and cut through the grass, still dewy in the frigid morning air, to where Baba stands on the steps. He's typing into his phone and looks up in surprise as he sees us approaching. Without saying a word, he pulls Mustafa and me into a tight embrace for what seems like a long time before letting us go. When he speaks, his face is full of sadness.

"It's devastating. We poured so many years of our lives into building this place. I painted those walls for the first time with my own hands, and now it's been . . ." His voice cracks and he stops.

I swallow hard. I can't remember ever seeing my father this upset. Baba seems to become aware of me and tries to smile in my direction.

"Don't worry, geeta. Everything will be okay." Baba rubs my back. "You should have left the kids at home," he adds quietly to Mama. "This is no place for them to be right now."

"You're right." Mama's eyes are glassy. "I just wanted to keep them close to me. Mustafa, can you please take your sister and wait in the car?"

Mustafa takes the keys without a word, and I follow him back to the car, while our parents look for Imam Malik and Hamid Uncle in the mosque.

We sit in the front seats, the dark leather already cold

through my jeans even though the car has only been off for a few minutes. Mustafa puts the key in the ignition and turns on the heat and the stereo. I can feel the warm air blowing, but it doesn't seem to make a difference as my teeth chatter from something other than the cold. Plus the upbeat pop song playing through the speakers seems oddly disrespectful. Mustafa switches it off, and we wait without saying a word. My mind floods with a million questions about what is going on, but I know Mustafa doesn't have the answers, and the look on his face warns me to stay quiet.

As the minutes creep by, and our parents aren't in sight, Mustafa starts to fidget. He checks his hair in the rearview mirror, examines the start of a pimple on his chin, puts his hood up, and slouches in the seat, drumming his fingers on the steering wheel.

"I can't sit here any longer. I'm going to check out what happened," he finally says. "You coming?"

"Mama said to wait here."

"Well, you can wait if you want." And with that, Mustafa jumps out of the car. I scramble to follow him, my heart pounding again with a mix of fear and nervousness. Together, we run across the wet grass and up the steps to the community building.

Mustafa pulls open the carved green door of the community hall. I take a deep breath, like I'm about to go underwater, and slowly enter the foyer. Its small sofa, side table filled with pamphlets and flyers, and a few chairs look pretty much the same as always. *Maybe things won't be as bad as I imagined.* But, then, as we continue into the main hall, I gasp.

It's unrecognizable, as if a tornado swept through, picked up furniture, and threw it against the walls. Tables and chairs are turned upside down, and the floor is littered with cracked frames. I recognize them as the calligraphy that a local Moroccan painter recently donated. Two wood display cases are knocked onto their sides, and all the treasures from around the Muslim world are broken and scattered. The microphone and podium on the stage, where I heard a presentation by a children's book illustrator a few weeks earlier, are destroyed.

Something in my chest breaks into pieces as I survey the room. Worst of all are the walls, once creamy white, now covered with black spray paint. My eyes scan the hateful phrases written in thick, crooked lines—sloppy writing that screams *Go Home*, *Terrorists*, *Towelheads*, and bad words so terrible that I squeeze my eyelids shut tight. The writing cuts deep, as the fear of whoever could do something like this grips me. I reach for Mustafa, feeling dizzy, and realize that I'm holding my breath.

"Are you okay?" he whispers. "You look like you're going to puke."

I nod but hold Mustafa's hand tightly as we walk down the hall past the bathrooms. As we pass the little library, one of my favorite parts of the Islamic Center, I see that the books have been knocked off the shelves and many are in shreds. I peek in horror, unable to bear the thought of anyone mishandling the Holy Quran—tearing out the pages and apparently stomping on them. Mustafa mutters under his breath, and his eyes seem darker than usual as he scans the room.

"Let's get out of here," he says. "I can't see any more."

As we step outside into the cool air, we both take deep breaths.

"Who would do this?" I finally ask when I can.

"I wish I knew!" Mustafa's voice is thick with anger. He bites his lip.

"I thought we asked you to stay in the car." Baba sounds reproachful as he hurries toward us from the side of the building.

"You were taking so long, we got worried," Mustafa says. I can tell he's trying his best not to cry.

"Did you go inside?" Baba asks.

"Yeah," Mustafa mutters. "Do the cops know who did this?"

"I wish you had listened to us," Baba says. "It's cold out here, but come wait with us for a few more minutes. I don't want you to go into the mosque building, do you hear me? It's wet and smoky and a mess in there . . . and the police are still collecting evidence."

We nod. The last thing either of us wants is to go into the mosque and see more destruction.

We follow Baba to where Mama and Thaya Jaan are talking to Hamid Uncle and a couple of other people who have arrived. Imam Malik is standing aside speaking to a police officer and a reporter. A van labeled CHANNEL 7 NEWS arrived while they were inside. I spot blue-checkered pajamas under Imam Malik's brown leather jacket and figure that he rushed out of his house as soon as he heard what had happened.

I would have laughed with Mustafa about that if this weren't all so terrible.

"Let's go," Mama says wearily as she sees us. She seems distracted and says to no one in particular, "I just can't believe that this happened."

I don't want to believe it either. All I want is to crawl back into bed and wake up again, to find out that all of it was just a bad dream. Hamid Uncle clears his throat loudly and doesn't acknowledge us, which is very out of character.

"It's going to be hundreds of thousands of dollars in repairs between both buildings." He pushes his glasses up his nose. "Maybe even more if they find out there was structural damage."

"But it could have been so much worse," Salma Auntie says. "If that person in a passing car hadn't noticed the smoke and called the fire department, and if they hadn't come so quickly, the entire building could have burned to the ground."

"I know," Mama says. "We'll have to try to be grateful, but it's hard. This just feels so violating, and terrifying. I thought we were part of this community, and now to think that someone wanted to . . ." Mama looks down at me and stops talking.

Imam Malik shakes hands with the reporter and walks over to us. Tons of other cars are pulling into the parking lot now, and I want to tell them to turn around and go home and not go inside the Islamic Center.

"Assalaamwalaikum." Imam Malik's usually smiling face is drooping. "What a nightmare."

"What are the police saying?" Mama asks. "Do they know who did this?"

"The police are opening a full investigation, but it's going to take time before we get any answers."

"What if they come back?" I ask.

Imam Malik pats me on the shoulder. "Don't worry. The people who did this are shameless cowards. They won't dare to come back. And even if they try, we are working with the police to set up additional security."

"We have to catch them. Whoever did this can't just get away with it!" Mustafa speaks to the ground and acts like something is in his eyes. "They need to pay for what they did."

"I'm angry too, but let's be patient. We'll see what happens," Imam says gently as he puts his arm around Mustafa. "Leave it in the hands of God and the police, who are working hard."

"Any idea how long before we can reopen, realistically?" Mama asks.

"It's going to be many weeks, if not months." Imam shakes his head sadly.

"We are going to have to let all the groups we invited to our events know that they won't be happening anymore," Mama adds.

The Quran competition! For weeks I've been dreading it, but now that it's being snatched away, I'm surprised by how badly I want it back. I think about how excited all my friends have been about the cotton candy and the dunk tank, and how hard everyone has been working to prepare. And I suddenly feel cheated and angry.

"Yes, if you could please notify everyone, it would be helpful—and one less thing for me to manage right now." Imam Malik shifts his weight as if the burden resting on him is too much to carry. "Now, I'm sorry, I have to go speak to the others who have arrived." He puts his hand over his chest and then rushes off.

We wait while our parents finish their conversations. It's only when my stomach starts growling fiercely that I remember we haven't eaten anything all morning. Finally, we head back to the car, and as we walk, I catch up to Mustafa and tug on his arm.

"What?" he asks without stopping.

"I was praying that I didn't have to be in the Quran competition," I whisper. I don't want anyone else to hear me.

"And?"

"And . . . look what happened." I wave my hand around, pointing toward the buildings.

"What?" Mustafa snorts. "Don't be ridiculous. It doesn't work like that. This has nothing to do with you."

I stand in place, blinking rapidly.

"Listen." Mustafa's voice is softer, and he stops walking. "Did you spray-paint those walls or set that fire?"

I shake my head.

"Then it's not your fault. Okay? Some really evil people did that."

"Do you think they will catch them?"

"I hope so." Mustafa scowls. "It's just so freaking unfair. What kind of person would want to destroy a place where people gather to pray and learn?"

I don't want to think about it. I don't want to think about who they were, and why they were smashing things or spraying the walls. Instead I just pray for things to go back to the way they were before, back to before this horrible night, back to before I wished my way out of the competition, back to before I heard Thaya Jaan say what he did about music, and back to before I messed everything up with Soojin and Emily. The heaviness that has settled around my heart is getting to the point where it is slowly being crushed. I'm afraid I will never feel normal again.

22

"Turn it up." Salma Auntie hands Mustafa the remote control with a frustrated scowl. "I can't figure this thing out."

I'm squished in the middle of the sofa between Hamid Uncle and Mama as everyone crowds around the TV in the family room, waiting for the five o'clock news to begin. Even though it isn't even dark outside yet, after all the early morning drama at the Islamic Center, it seems much later than it actually is. I'm glad that the house has filled up with friends. After we came home in the morning, we quietly ate leftovers from the party the night before, which felt like a million years ago. Then we went upstairs to try to nap. I lay in bed, trying to ignore the phone ringing constantly, and replayed everything I'd seen that morning in my head. The words "Terrorists" and "Go Home!" kept flashing through my mind, and a flood of feelings—fear, anxiety, anger—clouded my thoughts. *I am home. Where else would I go?*

A few hours later, Rabiya rang the doorbell. She was holding a large white bowl covered in foil, and Salma Auntie stood behind her carrying a big tray.

"Put these in the kitchen," Auntie said after kissing me on the forehead. I remembered that Salma Auntie always cooked massive amounts of food when she was stressed out. The bowl was filled with vegetable rice, and the tray held meat pastries.

Imam Malik arrived with his family soon after. He had changed out of his pajamas into jeans, but the sadness and worry hadn't left his eyes. I could see it even when I tickled baby Sumaiya, making her shriek with laughter. She lunged for me and touched my cheeks with her chubby fingers, like it was just any other day.

The grown-ups settled into the living room and launched into a long conversation about the details of what had happened that morning. Their voices were somber as they compared notes, but at times someone would speak loudly in anger. While they talked, they drank the chai that Mustafa and I made and mindlessly chewed on tea biscuits and dried fruit and nuts. We all hovered around our parents, preferring to be nearby instead of playing in the basement like usual. I sat on the bench of my piano since all the other seats were taken.

"Shh," shushes Auntie, "it's starting." Mustafa turns the volume on the TV even louder.

Everyone quiets down and stares at the blond woman on the screen, the same reporter we'd seen that morning. "We're here at the scene of a serious attack of vandalism and arson at the Islamic Center of Greater Milwaukee," the woman says.

The camera pans through the destruction of the community building and then swings right to show the mosque. Somehow, the scene appears even worse on camera and almost unreal, like a war zone. I gasp when I see the images of the interior of the mosque, which is charred and almost unrecognizable. The once gold-trimmed panels are covered with soot, and the carpet is blackened. Imam Malik is walking through the mosque, pointing at the ceiling, which has been damaged by flames, and talking with a police officer, who is then interviewed about the arson.

"We don't have any suspects at this time, but we are asking the community to please come forward with any information that can lead us to whoever committed these crimes." The officer stands stiffly and speaks directly into the camera.

The reporter next asks Imam Malik questions about the history of the Islamic Center, and his voice shakes as he answers. And then, as quickly as it started, the story is over. The anchors switch to news about a rash of robberies in a neighborhood on the other side of town. Mustafa turns off the TV, and everyone sits quietly with grim expressions on their faces.

"The police have been taking this seriously." Thaya Jaan

breaks the silence. I'm surprised to hear his voice. Even though his face shows that he's very troubled by everything that has happened, he hasn't said much about it.

"Muslims have far more friends than enemies in this country. Some people don't understand Islam or are misled and fear us. But I'm getting so many calls of support from our friends and neighbors in the community," Imam Malik says.

"It's true," Hamid Uncle adds. "Even with things like this, I'm still convinced there's no better place to be a Muslim in the world than in this country."

I think about what Baba said about Thaya Jaan wishing our family had gone back to Pakistan and worrying that his brother wouldn't like our lives in America. But Thaya Jaan, surprisingly, nods in agreement.

"There are many things about life here in America that are very good," Thaya Jaan says. "And I'm starting to think you may be right."

I shift on the bench, and my elbow strikes one of the

piano keys. The sound startles everyone, who are already jumpy and on edge.

"Why don't you play us something, geeta," Baba suggests. "It might help." When I look at him with surprise he gives me a sly look.

I hesitate and glance at Thaya Jaan to see his reaction. He doesn't say anything and only smiles slightly. *Did Baba already talk to him about music like he said he would?*

"Go on," Mama pushes. "It'll be good for us to take our minds off of everything."

I spin around to face the piano, glad to be doing something other than just sitting, listening, and worrying. As I run my fingers over the smooth keys, a warm, comforting feeling settles over my shoulders and moves down my arms. I flip through the songs I've been practicing in my lesson book and decide on Beethoven's Sonata number 8. I take a deep breath and start to play, letting my emotions pour out through my fingertips.

After the first few measures, I forget everything for a

moment and feel whole again, in spite of what happened earlier in the day. I play as if no one is listening, basking in the richness of the sound. Finally, as I hit the last note, I remember that I'm not alone and turn around.

Baby Sumaiya squeals and bangs her toy on the coffee table, drooling with a big toothless grin. But everyone else has tears in their eyes—even Thaya Jaan.

23

My school cafeteria is packed with people. They are sitting in rows of chairs facing a microphone set up on one end of the room. Imam Malik and a police officer stand side by side and are taking turns answering questions. Baba and Hamid Uncle sit behind them.

It feels strange to be in the school at night, since I skipped during the day. Mama let me stay home after she saw how wiped out I was in the morning. I hadn't been able to sleep last night either and had bad dreams about what had happened at the Islamic Center. Mustafa ended up staying home too, and we both helped to spread the word about the meeting that Mama and others had set up with county officials. The rest of the day I watched three hours of sitcom reruns on television until my head started to hurt. Now, at night, I realize that I'm going to be missing *The Voice* and wonder if my favorite contestant, Javier, will make it to the next round.

The cafeteria is filled with faces I recognize from the community, like Dahlia and her parents, Sami's family, and Sister Naima and her husband. And there are so many others who have come, like Pastor Stevens, Rabbi Weiss, local officials, my principal, and a bunch of teachers from my school and the others in the county. Mrs. Barton is sitting next to a man I recognize from the photos on her desk as her husband. And Ms. Bixler and Mr. Nelson are there too. Ms. Holly sits in the row behind them, her usual smiling face drawn and tight. But when she meets my eye, she gives me a sympathetic look.

Everyone in the room is bursting with questions, which Officer Jenkins nervously answers, his face red under a crew cut. I feel sorry for him as he struggles to explain things that are unexplainable. A lady, elegant in her bright pink-and-purple-printed African dress with a matching head wrap stands up, her body stiff with anger.

"Our center is known for being active in the community—we work with local charities and have a free health clinic. We help people. So I just don't understand *why*. Why would someone want to do this to us?"

Officer Jenkins shifts, and his face grows even redder.

"Our best guess is that this was a simple act of hate. We don't believe that anyone specific in the community was targeted. Whoever did this was looking to send a message of fear, aimed at all Muslims." Several people murmur in agreement.

It worked. I'm scared.

An older man with graying hair in a suit stands next.

"Have you made any arrests yet?"

"I'm afraid not," Officer Jenkins replies as he mops his brow with a napkin. "We are exploring all the leads we have, and we will keep you informed."

My head starts to ache again.

"We have time for one more question," Imam Malik

says as a flurry of hands fly up. He points to Sami's mom, who has been waiting.

"I just want to know how we can make sure this won't happen again. How can we feel safe in the future?"

Imam Malik nods toward Officer Jenkins, who says, "We are working with the leadership to set up additional security measures at the Islamic Center, including a more sophisticated surveillance and alarm system. We also need everyone to be extra vigilant for any suspicious activity."

"Thank you, Officer Jenkins, for taking the time to talk with us tonight. Let's give the kind officer a round of applause," Imam Malik says.

Officer Jenkins holds up his hands as the applause starts. "Before I leave, I just want to say I know that this a terrible, challenging time for the Muslim community here in Milwaukee. On behalf of the entire police force, I can say that we are all deeply saddened by this hate crime. It's simply unacceptable, and it's un-American. We will do whatever we can to prevent anything like this from happening in the future and to make sure justice is served."

Everyone's applause grows louder.

"Thank you, Officer, for all that you are doing to get to the bottom of this and keep our community safe," Imam Malik says again. "If everyone else can stick around for a few more minutes, we need to talk about the cleanup effort and ways you can help."

I rub my eyes, finally feeling sleepy. I'm sitting next to Thaya Jaan, who's nodding off in his seat. The people who are standing in front of the door move to the side, and it opens again. I blink a few times when I see Soojin's mom walk in, and right behind her is Mr. Park and Soojin. With them is a tall man with blond hair.

Mama is sitting near the door, and she quickly rises to greet them. She gives Mrs. Park and Soojin hugs and shakes hands with the others. I sit glued to my seat, wondering what to do. *Does Soojin want to talk to me?* I'm still sitting there, debating with myself, as Mama motions for me and Thaya Jaan to come over.

"Hi, Amina dear," Mrs. Park says as I approach them. "We're so sorry to hear about what happened at the mosque."

"We wanted to come earlier to offer our support but got delayed at the restaurant," Mr. Park adds.

"Thank you so much." I hug each of them and give Soojin a sideways glance, uncertain about what to say or do. But Soojin comes closer and gives me a big hug, squeezing me tight.

"Are you okay?" she asks with worry in her eyes. "This is so scary, and so crazy."

"Yeah," I gulp as a flood of relief rushes through me. *Soojin's acting like her regular self.*

"We saw the story on TV. I can't imagine what it would be like to have something like this happen at our church."

I nod. "I wanted to call you and tell you right away."

"You should have."

I pause. "I felt too bad about everything that happened at school. I'm really sorry."

"It's okay." Soojin shakes her head slightly as if she wants to dismiss the thought.

"It's not okay," I insist. I play with the zipper of my jacket, and the words come rushing out. "It was wrong of me to say anything about Emily. I should have known better and been more careful and—"

"Don't worry about it." Soojin cuts me off. "That doesn't matter right now." She waves her hand around the room.

"But I have been worried about it. At the same time that I've been worried about all of this." I can't let any more time go by before clearing the air. "I hope you can trust me again."

Soojin pauses.

"I can, Amina. I know you. I'm sorry too. For yelling at you."

I nod, too relieved to speak. The handsome blond man introduces himself to Mama and Thaya Jaan next. "I'm Mark Heller," he says, flashing a set of perfect teeth. "I'm here to offer my help." *Heller? Could it possibly be?*

"Are you Emily's dad?" I blurt out.

"Yes, that's me. Emily was very upset by what happened. She told me last night what good friends you are. I heard about this meeting and decided to stop by on my way home." He smiles at me, and I notice that his green eyes are the exact same shade as Emily's.

"Thank you," I manage to squeak. *After all that happened, Emily said we were good friends?*

"It's the least I can do," Mr. Heller continues. "What happened is just appalling. We all have to stick together in times like these."

Everyone murmurs in agreement.

"I own a construction company," Mr. Heller continues, addressing Mama. "And I'd like to offer my services to help your community rebuild. I can do the repairs at cost, and only charge for materials and labor."

"Wow, that's so nice of you," I interrupt. A wave of gratitude washes over me, and my eyes fill with tears.

"Yes, that is an extremely generous offer. Let me introduce you to the others." Mama wipes her eyes too and smiles widely as she leads Mr. Heller toward Imam Malik and Baba. Mr. Heller places a firm hand on my shoulder as he walks by.

"Everything is going to be okay," he says.

I nod, my heart full again, but in a good way this time. I pull Soojin, who's been listening to everything, over to a couple of empty chairs along the wall.

"Did you hear that?" I say. "I haven't been nice to Emily at all, and now . . . her dad is being so great."

"She's not a bad person, Amina. I think we just saw her hanging around with Julie before and thought she was like her. She's actually—"

"I know. She's nice. I was so worried about Emily becoming friends with you that I didn't notice she was trying to be friends with me, too."

"It's okay, Amina. I think she still wants to be friends with you."

"Do you think she's still mad at me?"

"No. I talked to her about it later. She got your note. And she believes that you weren't trying to hurt her or anything. She's okay."

I hug my friend again, so glad that she came. The meeting has wrapped up, and people are standing together in small groups talking. Mustafa is stacking empty chairs with Yusuf and putting them away. Imam Malik and Baba are talking to Mr. Heller. *He's right,* I think. *Everything is going to be okay. Insha'Allah.*

"Hey!" I remember suddenly. "How was the swearing-in? I should have said congratulations to you and your parents."

"It was really cool! We were with all these people who moved to the US from all over the world." Soojin described the hall and the way it all worked. "So, I guess it's official!" she adds. "We're going to have the party in a couple weeks."

"So . . . should I call you Susan now?"

"Well, not yet." Soojin's grin is slightly sheepish. "After all that, when it was time to sign the final papers, I just couldn't imagine not being Soojin anymore. Kind of like you said."

"Wait, so you're going to stay Soojin?"

"For now. I don't feel like a Susan just yet." Soojin giggles. "But who knows? Maybe I'll feel like a Natasha later!"

"Or maybe a Fiona!" I laugh.

"Oh no, never a Fiona. I was just humoring Emily. No ogre names for me!"

Mrs. Park walks up and holds out her hand. "Come on, girls. A long day like this calls for some frozen custard.

I asked your mom, Amina, and she said you can come to Kopp's with us."

Sweet! I take her hand and pull up Soojin behind me. As much as I love the creamy dessert and loading it up with all my favorite toppings, the idea of spending time with my best friend again is even better. It sounds like the perfect plan.

24

The room is cavernous, with high, slanted ceilings and exposed wooden beams that give me the feeling of being in a giant barn. At one end is a small stage with colorful hand-made quilts hanging on either side of a giant gold cross. The stage holds a podium with two big potted trees on either side of it and a large bouquet of pink and white roses in front. A line of tall windows directs rectangular beams of light on the polished and shiny pews.

I inhale deeply, trying to appear calm even though my heart thumps wildly as I walk up the steps to the stage, where Imam Malik is standing. He gives me an encouraging nod and steps to the side of the podium, allowing me to take my place behind it. The microphone on the podium is a little too high for me to speak into, so I adjust it just below my mouth. *Don't forget to breathe.*

And then I find the courage to take a peek into the huge crowd seated in front of me.

The room is packed with faces, most of them familiar. My parents, Mustafa, and Thaya Jaan are sitting with Rabiya's family on one side of the room. Behind them sit Sister Naima and her family. In front of them are a smiling Soojin and the rest of the Park family. Next to Soojin I see Emily and Mr. and Mrs. Heller.

I smile and unfold a piece of paper with the words I had typed out earlier and try to ignore the trembling in my hands. When my brain manages to command my hands to stay still, my leg starts to quiver, but at least it's hidden from view behind the podium. *You can do this. Relax.*

"Assalaamwalaikum. My name is Amina Khokar, and I'm going to recite surah Fatiha for you today," I begin. "But first I want to thank my friend Soojin Park and her parents, Mr. and Mrs. Park, for generously arranging to have our

Quran competition here at the Milwaukee Central Presbyterian Church."

Everyone claps and cheers for the Parks, and Mr. and Mrs. Park bow their heads. It was only two weeks earlier that I came up with the idea of hosting the competition at the church Soojin's family attends. Soojin thought it was a great plan, and we asked her parents, who are on the steering committee of the church, for their help. The committee overwhelmingly agreed and even pitched in to the college fund for the winner.

Imam Malik happily accepted the offer to host the competition. And then they decided to open up the lawn for the interfaith carnival and raise funds for rebuilding. Even with Mr. Heller leading the efforts to rebuild the mosque and community center, it was going to be months before it would open. My school championed the carnival planning, led by Ms. Holly, who formed committees of students and volunteers from the local synagogue and Emily's church. She also got a music school to set up a stage outside, where our band and chorus would hold a winter concert dress rehearsal.

"Always take any chance you get to perform in front of an audience," Ms. Holly told our class.

And now, just a couple of weeks later, everything came together and was finally happening on a beautiful, cool, sunny November afternoon.

I don't recognize my own voice as it echoes through the speakers. I'm the first of fifteen students competing, since each participating Islamic school program entered five top contestants. At home a week earlier, I finally confided to the imam about how panicked I was about speaking in front of a crowd.

"Does this have something to do with John Hancock?" he asked with a small smile.

"Yeah. What should I do?"

"How about if you go first?" Imam Malik suggested.

"What? First? How does that help?"

"You won't have to sit through the other students speaking," he explained. And then he encouraged me to recite the opening verses of the Quran. Not only is it the first passage that I learned as a child, but since I utter them in every prayer, it makes it less likely that I'll freeze and forget my lines.

"You know, I still get really nervous every time I speak in front of an audience," Imam Malik confessed.

"You? But you do it all the time." I was shocked. The imam delivers the weekly Friday sermon, speaks every Sunday, and gives lectures regularly. He always seems so relaxed standing in front of a group, like it's one of his favorite things to do.

"I know," Imam Malik explained. "But even still, every time before I start to talk, my palms sweat and my nerves kick in. I've just learned to ignore it and to push through. Because once I start speaking, I realize that it's going to be okay."

My throat starts to dry up as I stand on the stage and study everyone who has come together to help my community. *Just push through, like Imam said.* I wait for the applause for the Parks to die down and continue to speak.

"Surah Fatiha," I start. "The Opening." And then I recite the words I learned as soon as I could put sentences together. Even though I've said them thousands of times in my life, over the past week I worked with Thaya Jaan to focus on the sounds of each letter with the rules of Quranic pronunciation. I stare at the Arabic letters on the page, imagining them as musical notes in my piano book. My voice is like the keys, following the instructions of the letters, vowels, and other signals on the page. In this way, with my vocal cords as my instrument, I glide through the verses, wavering slightly at first, but getting stronger as I continue. As I speak, I think of the meaning of the words that praise God for his gifts and protection and seek his guidance to overcome every difficulty.

"Ameen." I finish and quickly hurry off the stage through the applause, back to my seat between Soojin and Emily. I spot Ms. Holly in a rear pew, and she gives me a big "okay" sign.

"Good job," Emily whispers. Her eyes are shining. "That sounded amazing."

I smile at her, surprised by how easy it is to think of Emily as a friend already. The day after the community meeting, when Mr. Heller came to make his fantastic offer of support, I went into school early and found Emily in the gym before the bell rang. I didn't even have to deliver the long apology I had practiced at home—Emily saw me and, like Soojin, gave me a hug and said how sad she was about what had happened at the Islamic Center. She didn't even want to talk about Justin or Bradley or how sorry I was for blurting out her secret. That was history. I still felt guilty for what I had done but promised myself that I would never betray a friend's trust again.

The next contestant is a tiny boy, hardly seven or eight years old, with a neat bow tie and hair that hangs over his eyes. He walks confidently to the stage. As he recites a short surah, I'm jarred by the power of his voice. He takes a deep bow when he's done. And then it's Mustafa's turn. My brother is dressed the nicest I've seen him in a long time— looking sharp in tan slacks and a maroon button-down shirt. His hair is gelled in his messy style, and he's freshly shaved. I hear some girls whispering and wonder if they're talking about how cute he is.

Mustafa is reciting a passage of the Quran that I don't know. He's kept his promise to the imam and, after he was caught skipping Sunday school, has been taking his participation in the competition more seriously. And he's been working with Thaya Jaan many nights long after I go to bed.

What I don't expect is how much Mustafa sounds like a younger version of our uncle. His voice rings clear and steady, filling the church with lyrical notes and giving me goose bumps. A few moments after he starts speaking, I realize my jaw has dropped and my mouth is actually open. I don't want to make him laugh and quickly shut it as he continues to masterfully glide through the verses. His face is serene, and he only glances at the open book in front of him occasionally.

My brother never sings around me. Ever. And even though he bought a used acoustic guitar last year, it's more for decoration and to act cool while strumming a chord than anything else. I've always assumed I'm the only one with musical talent between us. But I'm wrong.

"Mashallah," Baba whispers in the pew behind me, uttering the word used to praise in God's name.

I recognize the concluding phrases of Mustafa's passage that refer to forgiveness and God's mercy. And then he finishes and bows slightly while the room bursts into thunderous applause. I join in, clapping the loudest. *I'd hate to be the one going next.*

The last contestant is a thirteen-year-old girl from Sheboygan, who is also really good as she recites the final verses of the Quran. And then everyone waits for the judges from each of the participating schools to decide the winners. The room pulses with nervous energy. Finally, Imam Malik runs back up to the stage, looking flustered and excited at once. He announces the third- and second-place winners, two students from the other schools—a tall girl with braces and the bow-tie boy with the big voice. When it's time to announce the first-place winner, I hold my breath as the imam says, "And the winner is our very own . . . Mustafa Khokar."

I turn around in my seat and see Baba clap Mustafa on the shoulder as my brother looks up, genuinely stunned. I grin at him, and his face slowly spreads into a wide smile as he realizes what's happening. With a wink for me, he walks up to the stage, shaking his head like he can't quite believe it. My heart swells with pride as I watch Mustafa shake Imam Malik's hand and accept a big gold trophy with an open book on top. Next he takes the theme park tickets, holding up the envelope and ducking his head as he says thank you into the microphone. But then, as Imam Malik hands him the college money, Mustafa leans into the microphone again.

"I'd like to donate part of this to help set up a little kids' basketball league at the Islamic Center when it reopens," he says, and the room erupts into cheers. His cheeks turn redder as he continues to speak quickly, waving his hands to settle everyone down.

"We'll use it to buy equipment," he says. "I'm sure some of my friends from the Greendale team will help me coach."

My brother looks more confident and sure of himself with every word he says. I'm certain he and his team are going to be a huge success.

25

"Go on! Give it your best shot! You can't get—" SPLASH! The small seat he's perched on gives way, and Imam Malik falls into the water. He comes up sputtering and shivering, even though he's wearing a wet suit and scuba goggles, while Sami dances around him and trash-talks.

"Oh yeah!" he cackles. "I got you."

"The imam is so great." Soojin laughs from where she stands next to Rabiya and Dahlia.

"Yeah. You're so lucky that you're part of such an amazing community," Emily adds.

"So are you guys," I say as I look around at all the different people from their churches who have gathered together.

The carnival is spread out across the expansive church lawn, and parents and friends work at a dozen booths. Justin and his mom are running the bean bag toss. I spot Bradley handing out prizes for a basketball-shooting game.

Mustafa and Yusuf are standing next to Baba, all three chowing on bulgogi piled high on paper plates that the Park Avenue Deli is supplying through the Parks' new food truck. Mr. Park's two assistants are having trouble keeping up with the line. The food section has the usual vendors selling samosas and kabob rolls, and a big cotton candy machine. A few parents stand behind a long table and sell homemade baked goods, including Emily's mom, who passes out her peanut butter cookies.

I catch Thaya Jaan, who has passed on a kabob roll, sinking his teeth into a jumbo cheeseburger. Mustafa finally managed to win him over to American food, and the two have shared a couple of late-night pizzas over the past few weeks. Thaya Jaan rushed over to us with Mama and Baba after the Quran competition program was over and hugged us both tightly.

"I'm so proud of you." His eyes crinkled around the edges more than usual.

"Did you two remember to thank Thaya Jaan for all of his hard work with you?" Mama asked quickly.

"No need," Thaya Jaan said. "I've learned as much from them as they have from me." He put his arm around Baba.

"You both have done an excellent job raising these children," he added. I watched my father stand taller from the praise and knew how much it meant to him.

The big stage is set up across from the food vendors, where the Greendale High School jazz band fills the air with classic tunes. I recognize one of Mustafa's friends playing the alto saxophone and a boy from his basketball team strumming the bass guitar. Ms. Holly is standing to the side, talking to the high school band teacher. The sixth graders are going to do the Blast from the Past rehearsal next. I can pick out the band and chorus members spread out around the lawn in their various forms of black pants and white shirts. Justin showed up wearing black track pants and a white sweatshirt that is already covered with grass stains.

"Come on." Soojin pulls my hand. "The line for the bounce house isn't long right now. Let's get in before it's time for the rehearsal."

I motion to Emily, Rabiya, and Dahlia, and we all run over to the giant inflated castle. I stop, thinking, while my friends kick off their shoes.

"Go ahead without me. I'll be right back."

And then I run back over to where Ms. Holly is standing and whisper in her ear. Ms. Holly nods enthusiastically.

I run back to the bounce house and dive in, feeling lighter than I have in weeks as I jump. Soojin leaps and twirls and does a cartwheel. Rabiya tries to do splits and ends up falling on me, knocking me over.

"I think it's time." Emily strains to hear the announcement over the whir of the air pump. "We'd better go back. I have to get my clarinet."

She slides out of the castle, smooths her white sweaterdress over her leggings, and adjusts her headband. Soojin slips her black ballet flats back on and looks at me.

"What's the matter? Are you nervous about playing the piano in front of everyone?" she asks.

"No, I think I'll be okay." I've practiced enough to play the songs in my sleep.

We walk up to the stage as Ms. Holly introduces the grade and explains the program to the crowd. I climb onto the stage and settle onto the piano bench, feeling instantly relaxed as my fingers rest on the keys. On Ms. Holly's signal, I launch into the medley of songs and the chorus sings along. As I start the 1960s songs, I wonder if Baba is humming along too. When I'm halfway through the 1970s portion, Ms. Holly slips onto the bench beside me and starts to play, and I quickly stand up. I walk to the center of the stage, lift the microphone off the stand, and raise it to my lips.

I look out into the audience, but it is a blur of faces. Instead I focus on the cool breeze on my face and on the bright blue sky, where I train my eyes on a cloud. As Ms. Holly hits the starting note, I ignore the trembling in my leg, find my voice, and hear myself softly and clearly sing the words to my very first solo.

"I was born by the river in a little tent . . ."

There's a smattering of applause and cheering. I take a deep breath and continue a little louder, "And just like that river I've been running ever since . . ." My legs are steadier now, and I start to sway slightly to the music.

"It's been a long time, a long time coming . . ." I begin to recognize the faces in the audience. I find Mama, Baba, Mustafa, and Thaya Jaan, all smiling, and Rabiya, whistling like crazy. And then, suddenly filled with happiness, I belt out the words I know are true with all my might: "But I know a change gonna come. Oh yes it will."

And I'm ready for it.

A Reading Group Guide to

Amina's Voice

By Hena Khan

About the Book

The first year of middle school is tricky. Suddenly, Amina's best friend, Soojin, starts talking about changing her name and, even worse, spending time with Emily—a girl who used to make fun of them! Amina's older brother seems to be getting into a lot of trouble for his grades, and now he wants to play basketball instead of studying. To make matters worse, her uncle comes to visit from Pakistan, and her parents seem to be trying awfully hard to impress him.

With so many changes, it's hard to know how to be a good friend, sister, and daughter. But when Amina's mosque is vandalized, she learns that the things that connect us will always be stronger than the things that try to tear us apart.

Discussion Questions

1. Describe Amina's feelings about music. What keeps Amina from telling her teacher that she would like to sing a solo? What could Amina do to overcome her fear? Have you ever been afraid to do something you wanted to do? What happened?

2. Why does Soojin consider changing her name? Why do you think Amina is uncomfortable with the idea of Soojin changing her name? Have you ever wanted to change your own name?

3. Why do you think Emily decides to stop being friends

with Julie and to start being friends with Soojin and Amina? Why doesn't Amina trust her at first? How would you react if someone who had been mean to you in the past tried to become your friend?

4. What causes tension between Amina's parents and her brother? How do they resolve their differences? Have you ever wanted to do something your parents did not want you to do? Have your parents ever required you to do something you did not want to do? How did you handle the situation?

5. How is Thaya Jaan related to Amina? How can you tell that Amina's parents respect Thaya Jaan? What do they agree about? What do they disagree about?

6. Why is Amina initially unhappy with the group she is assigned to work with on her class Oregon Trail project? What is the best thing about working with a group? What

is the hardest thing about working with a group? What does Amina learn from working with Bradley, Soojin, and Emily?

7. Describe what happens at Amina's Sunday School. Do you attend any religious services or classes? If so, how is Amina's experience similar to yours? How is it different?

8. Both Amina and Soojin have been teased because of the food they bring to school or the way their food smells. Why do you think people tease or bully kids who are different? If you were in Amina's or Soojin's position, how would you respond? If you encounter someone from a different cultural background, how should you respond to them?

9. Discuss the role that forgiveness plays in the novel. Who does Amina need to forgive? Who does she need to ask for forgiveness? Do you think it is more difficult to ask for forgiveness or to forgive someone else?

10. How does jealousy threaten Soojin and Amina's friendship? What does Amina learn about Soojin, Emily, and herself as a result? Do you think Soojin is a good friend to Amina? Is Amina a good friend to Soojin?

11. In the novel, Amina is trusted with secrets. Do you think she's right to keep Mustafa's secret? Should she have kept Emily's secret? Why is it sometimes hard to keep secrets? Are there ever secrets that you should not keep?

12. Amina's parents and Thaya Jaan disagree about whether or not music is forbidden. In every family, people disagree about the way to raise children and about what types of behavior should be allowed. How does Amina navigate the conflicting viewpoints in her own family? Have you ever had to navigate a similar situation? If so, how did you handle it?

13. What is backbiting? Why does Amina feel guilty of

backbiting? In your opinion, did she backbite Emily? Explain your answer.

14. Amina's parents are concerned that Thaya Jaan will not be happy when he visits because, as they say, "You know there's some bad feeling in this country toward Muslims, and all this negative talk in the news these days." When Thaya Jaan is in America, what evidence of bad feelings toward Muslims does he witness? What good things about America and acts of kindness does he witness? What does he conclude about life in America?

15. What is vandalism? How did the description of the vandalism of Amina's mosque make you feel? How do you think you would feel if your school or place of worship was vandalized? Explain how this act of violence ends up bringing Amina's community together.

16. The novel ends with a message of change. In literature,

characters that change are called *dynamic* characters. Almost all the characters in *Amina's Voice* are dynamic characters. Explain how each character changes.

Guide prepared by Amy Jurskis, English Department Chair at Oxbridge Academy in Florida.

This guide has been provided by Simon & Schuster for classroom, library, and reading group use. It may be reproduced in its entirety or excerpted for these purposes.

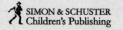

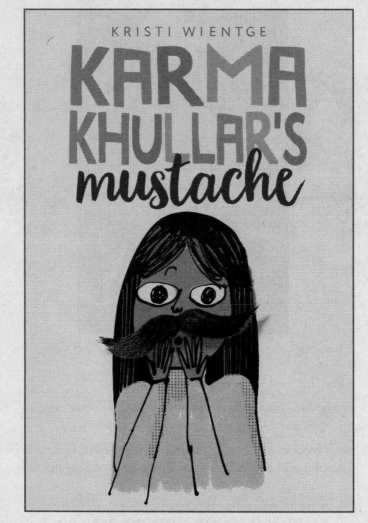

The wilder will teach the wolves how to be bold again, how to hunt and fight, and how to distrust humans. They teach them how to howl, because a wolf who cannot howl is like a human who cannot laugh."

"I loved the characters, the speed, the force of it all."
—PHILIP PULLMAN, author of *The Golden Compass*

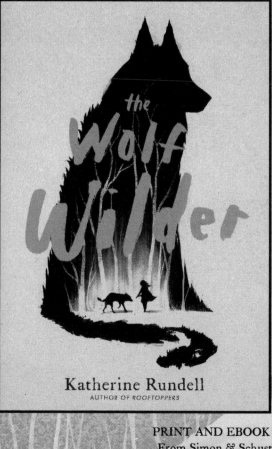

PRINT AND EBOOK EDITIONS AVAILABLE
From Simon & Schuster Books for Young Readers
simonandschuster.com/kids

Hena Khan is a Pakistani American who was born and raised in Maryland. She enjoys writing about her culture as well as all sorts of other subjects, from spies to space travel. She is the author of several books, including *It's Ramadan, Curious George*; *Golden Domes and Silver Lanterns*; and *Night of the Moon*. Hena lives in Rockville, Maryland, with her husband and two sons. You can learn more about Hena by visiting her website, henakhan.com.